Cain

"For it is foretold the Beast should bear an heir and the world would drown in blood. First born carries the Curse and with this Curse the earth will flood. Her sword is fierce and true, molded by fire and blessed by the Archangels. She carries the Light of the Sun and the Truth from the Heavens to restore what is lost. In the final hours, when the war between the Brothers of Light and the Brothers of Dark finds its way to earth, she will be called to lead. She is not the first but the last for it was her first mother who paved the path. Protectors, the Sons and Daughters of Seth will act as her guide, possessing gifts from the Heavens, this Huntress – for her they will fight. For this dark curse will roam the earth to and fro, and into the bowels of Hell he will go... for another heir will assume dominion once the curse is past until the final battle between what was first and what was last..."

Year: 2011 AD

City of Los Angeles

Cain inhaled the rich, husky sweet scent that haunted his senses for the last few months. Great. Just what he needed. He knew that this day would once again arrive. After all, he'd witnessed it time and time again. As a matter of fact, he was the very reason the Light sent a weapon of natural destruction against his kind. He sucked in another deep breath. His skin prickled and tingled as erotic chills coursed down his spine. Closing his eyes, he allowed himself to be consumed by the sheer force of it. The urge to seek her out intensified. He could easily begin the seduction, convince her to resent her caretakers and turn her against her very instincts.

However, this time around, it would not be so wise to make such a bold move.

Things were different. To make a direct move on a fledgling Huntress would be suicide, and with times being so uncertain with the "end of days" quickly approaching, there was a much bigger plan at stake.

"She is strong..." Cain heard himself say. Licking his lips, his fangs crested at the mere thought of her. Soon she would become a master manipulator of the elements; her thirst for his blood would surpass his own for human; angels would bow to her command and she would lead an army that Napoleon, Nero, and Julius himself would envy.

She was designed to be a masterpiece of warrior art. She would come to understand combat as she would lovemaking. Oh, to imagine her as a lover. Intense would hardly be the word to describe what she would be. Goddess of sensuality, Aphrodite, would not be able to hold a candle to her.

He had seen this in the Huntresses that came before this one, but the power that this particular Huntress emitted even at this distance was different.

"I do not know where you are sweet Huntress, but I will find you…soon…" he promised.

The Vampire Hunters Academy, the school for gifted humans and refuge for Guardians had not registered her in their books. Every Huntress born within the last two thousand years had attended that school. Those that came before that, he had to find the hard way. This only meant that the Guardians, those who were destined to protect her, had not found her yet.

Why?

Why would the Light not place her in the care of those most skilled to protect her until she could protect herself? What game was being played? The desire to hunt her, to taste her blood, to have her bend to his will became overwhelming. His gumline thickened, lengthening his fangs. Blood coursed to the baser regions of his body. Blood. That's what he needed. Her blood. Human blood.

He chuckled at the mere thought of it all; blood is where it began for him. Blood is what he paid for his ever-growing list of sins.

His story began in blood and he held the sneaking suspicion that blood is where his story would end.

He inhaled deeply, appreciating the chill of the night air from the rooftop that overlooked the city. The city's lights lit up the sky, while humans down below scurried about their meaningless and pointless lives. Licking his lips, he contemplated whom would be his next victim this night, while simultaneously wondering how the humans he fed on lived such short lives but the blood they provided offered him eternity?   Blood, his power, his pleasure, his pain – essentially his curse – he would forever remain bound to it. For eternity he would remain a slave to his more basic desires. He was a monster among men, a living breathing plague.

And it all began with blood…the blood of his brother Abel…

Chapter One

Year: 1. B.C.

"Brother, thou art the biggest fool in the history of fools," Cain murmured under his breath as he pushed through the thicket of foliage. The midday heat burned against his back, but he pressed on.

"Come on, Cain!" Abel laughed as he skipped ahead of him. "It will be fun!"

"Father said not to venture nearest The Garden," Cain yelled out behind his brother, who sprinted several meters ahead of him. "It's guarded, Abel!"

"The angels won't hurt us!" Abel yelled back. "They are not supposed to!"

"Not if they are—" Cain stopped running to catch his breath. Leaning forward with both hands on his knees, he groaned. "Abel!"

Abel's laughter could be heard through the trees and a after a few seconds, Cain took off running behind him. His brother always did this. Tempted fate at the hands of angels. But then when it was time for offering, he would somehow manage to find the best lamb, the best ox, and all of his offenses were forgiven. Cain shook his head at the thought.

Unbelievable.

They bypassed a family of monolithic trees, giants that were part of a collective group that Adam had referred to as The Nephilim Forest. Large thick branches spanned beyond the point of blotting out the harsh rays of the sun, headed in the direction of the never-ending sky. Cain hated this part of the land. He wished Abel would stop with the foolishness and simply do what father said. But no, his brother had to go gallivanting off like he was on some whimsical journey, chasing myths and legends like the buffoon no one cared to admit that he was.

"Ha, ha, ha!" Abel laughed victoriously as he reached the clearing- the same clearing that overlooked the lush greenery that offered an almost surreal environment of blues, greens, and golds. Large birds zig zagged about in the sky, their caws echoing well into the clearing in which the two young men stood.

"Do you see, Michael?" Abel asked, his honey brown eyes lit with excitement. "No one is guarding the entrance!"

"The cherubim could be there!" Cain hissed, his eyes searching the perimeter. "Our parents have already suffered dearly for their own crimes in The Garden. We shall not add to their transgressions!"

"Oh come on, Cain! He is forgiving and has proven so. He understands my need for adventure."

"There are rules, Abel!"

Abel casually pushed a stray hair from his face and eyed the outskirts of The Garden. The mystical fire swords reappeared out of the nothingness and slashed back and forth around the perimeter.

"Looks like its guardians have returned," Abel said coolly. "Oh, well. Another day then."

"Are you insane?" Cain growled.

Abel simply looked at his twin and offered a fully bellied laugh.

[5]

"Brother, you worry too much. I told you, He is forgiving!"

"Only for you…" Cain mumbled, looking away.

"He loves your offerings too," Abel said gently, approaching Cain. "Trust that He does."

Cain pulled away. "Let's just go before we find ourselves in more trouble."

"Cain! Abel? Come home!"

The two boys turned in the opposite direction of the clearing, towards their father's voice.

"Ach! Look what you've gotten us into now!" Cain grumbled as he turned around and started walking towards the trees. "Come on!"

"Here we come, father!" Abel shouted from behind Cain.

The two walked quickly in silence, with Cain lost in the fear of his father's ire. They were supposed to have been on a hunt, searching for the whereabouts of the lost cattle that wandered off a few days ago. So far, there had been no trace of said herd, and their small family was forced to eat whatever they could find. Cain thought about the harsh conditions under which they lived and wondered why his mother would have been so foolish, so naïve, so terribly stupid to allow herself to be tempted by the serpent. And his father…How could he not have possessed the discipline to not accept the fruit from Eve? His mother had been left to her own devices, unprotected by Adam, the angels, and everyone else. Darkness lurked in every corner of that beautiful garden. All because of one bad decision.

They were cast out to fend for themselves like common rodents.

Cain wished that he possessed the favor to speak with the Creator and demand to know why He went to such extremities, especially when Abel was so easy to forgive, despite his continuous offenses. What was it about Abel that was so special that he deserved grace and mercy? Everything that his parents did not deserve.

Everything that *he* did not deserve.

What made Abel worthy while everyone else was not?

A tall, dark masculine shadow greeted them a hundred yards away, and Cain instantly knew that it was Adam. Long, dark locks hung well past his waist as he stood with his chest bared. The goat skinned cloth that covered his loins blew with the breeze, while he gripped a long spear in his hand.

"Must you two always disobey?" Adam growled, once the two young men approached him.

"My apologies, father," Cain said, lowering his gaze.

"But, father," Abel began, his face still lit with excitement. "The Garden—"

"Is off limits," Adam stated firmly. "Stray too close and the cherubim will not discriminate. A trespasser is a trespasser."

Adam gently patted Abel on the back and playfully ruffled his locks. Cain did not overlook Adam's softening tone, or the slight smile when Abel skipped around being who he was.

Abel.

Cain could not put his finger on it, but as he hung back and slowly followed his father and brother. There was a difference in the way Adam treated them both. Cain swore that when he was old enough, he would blaze a path for himself on the other side of the world. So far in fact, that Adam nor his brother would have to worry about seeing him again. It'd become clear that Abel would forever be the most favored son.

Maybe he would be blessed to start a family of his own, and if he did, he vowed all of his children would feel the warmth of his love and know the pride in his eyes. He would never pat one son on the back and move forward while the other hung around in his shadow.

Chapter Two

"We are going to have move again," Adam announced around the campfire he built. "Towards the mountains this time."

"But mustn't we provide an offering of thanks first?" Eve asked as she continued to fiddle with her oldest daughter, Luluwa's thick, dark hair.

"Yes. The rains will be here soon and it would be best to perform the offerings before we move forward," Adam agreed.

Cain felt the gaze of his father on him as he sharpened the tip of the spearhead against the blunt stone. As always, his father would offer a stern reminder as to what he was to provide for an offering.

"Cain," Adam began. "What are you planning to present for your offering?"

The muscles in Cain's jawline tensed. He froze, instantly losing focus on the task at hand. "I will bring a ram. The biggest I can find." Cain tried to hide the tremble of uncertainty in his voice. He had messed up the last offering, and he vowed he would not make the same mistake again. Even if he had to spend days out in the sun, nights out in the cold, he would not rest until he brought down the largest male ram he could find.

"Good," Adam said after a beat, before turning to face Abel, who was busy staring off into the sky. "And what will you bring, son?"

"I am searching for the best of fruits, the best of what the earth produces," Abel declared. "He will be proud of what I find."

Adam gave Eve a knowing look. "Where do you plan on finding such fruit?"

"The angels will help me," Abel announced, still smiling. "They helped me the last time."

Eve smiled and shook her head, while Adam chuckled to himself. Cain continued sharpening his spear, ignoring his brother's lighthearted laughter. Their sister Luluwa appeared from behind them, carrying with her their youngest infant sister Aklia in her arms. The child was wrapped in goat skin. She greeted their parents warmly, but quickly took notice of Cain's sullen expression and sat next to him.

Cain adored his sister, and not just for her beauty. Her heart was kind, soft like their mother's. Her intellect was as sharp as their father's, but not as brutal. Her hand gently touched his, and instantly he found himself no longer able to focus on his spear. The eyes of their father burned against his back and he knew that Adam did not see him as fit for Luluwa's attentions. Luluwa was born a year after them, and still Adam had decided that Abel would make a better suitor instead of Cain.

"Luluwa," Adam's hard voice pierced through the darkness. "Go with your mother to prepare for bed.

"Yes, Father," Luluwa nodded. She stole a final glance at Cain and quickly ushered herself and her sister towards her mother, and Adam waited until the women disappeared behind the thicket.

"I will need for both of you to prepare," Adam said sternly. "Give your best," Adam said, his gaze shifting from Abel to Cain. "And you will have the best. Don't mess this up."

"We won't, Father," Abel asserted cheerfully.

Adam stood up, rising to his full six-foot-five frame. "Good. Be ready at sun rise."

Cain watched his father leave, headed in the direction of his mother and sisters before grumbling, "he hates me."

Abel looked at his brother, confused. "What are you talking about?"

"Nothing," Cain said with a sigh. "Just forget it." He dropped his spear and pushed himself up off of the large rock he had been sitting on and started sulking off in the other direction.

"Where are you going?" Abel asked as he attempted to follow behind his brother.

Cain raised his hand without looking at his brother. "Just leave me alone, Abel. I need some time to think."

"But, Father—"

"Leave me alone!" Cain shouted as he ran deeper into the trees.

He could hear Abel calling for him, begging him to return, but Cain refused to turn back. Adam, for whatever reason could not stand his presence. How could a father of twin sons despise one and love the other? What had he done other than spring forth from his mother's womb? How could he, the hunter, be forced to compete with a gatherer?

His brother frolicked and danced all day, making up songs, all the while searching for fruits and nuts. Meanwhile, Cain risked life and limb, spending days on the hunt. He sought after the largest of bulls, occasionally barely escaping with his own life. He understood the mindset of a predator. The hard beat of the heart against his rib cage, pounding like that of a drum. The rush as he closes in on the kill once his prey is in his sight. The tightness in his muscles as he crouches low like a lion in the tall grass. The beads of sweat that drip from his brow, down his chest and back all of this to provide the best meat to his family…all of this to provide what he considered his best offering. The blood of the strongest to show thanks, and to prove his loyalty to the One on High.

And yet, each time he brought back the blood of the strongest bull, his father would shake his head. Each time, he spent hours with his brother building the altar in preparation for the offering, only for his offer to be rejected. Nothing he did was good enough.

"This will be my last hunt for this offering," Cain murmured to himself once he finally plopped down on a fallen tree. Darkness surrounded him, and suddenly he missed the calming warmth of the campfire. But he would not go back. At least not now. "Maybe they won't miss me," he thought. "And maybe, I won't miss them." Leaning back onto the rotting bark, he closed his eyes and tried to ignore the cold.

Oh, but you will… came a soft melodic voice from the darkness.

Cain jumped up. "Who is that? Who are you?" he demanded, spinning around.

You will find out soon enough...the voice chuckled. *In the meantime, Adam and Eve await your return. Thank me later.*

Chapter Three

Cain wasn't sure how long he'd been sleep, but when he came to, he was still surrounded by darkness. Yawning, he pushed himself off of the rotting tree and stretched. No one came looking for him. Not surprising. Sucking in a deep breath, he knew it would be best to begin the hunt early. In two days, they would begin preparations for the Offering, and if he failed again...

He shook his head at the thought.

He moved through the thickets, careful to avoid the hard scratches from the thorny bushes that blocked his path as he made his way towards his family's camp site. As he reached the clearing, his skin tingled and instantly covered with gooseflesh. His senses alerted him to the presence of something dark. He spun around, and under the low light of the moon he witnessed the hulking form of a man. From what Cain could tell, hair as black as the lunar eclipse hung well below the entity's waist. However, it seemed as if the darkness grew denser around the form, leaving Cain unable to see his face.

"Who are you?" Cain demanded, wishing that he had not forgotten his spear at the camp site.

"Let's just say a friend," the entity stated softly. His deep baritone voice carried a soothing melody to it, that both calmed and unsettled Cain.

"How could you be a friend when I have never known you?" Cain asked, his eyes straining in the dark, desperate to see the entity's face.

"Let's just say I've known you, watched over you since your birth," the male said. "And I am here to help you."

Cain paused and then repeated, "Who are you?"

"You have an offering coming up," the entity stated, ignoring the question. "And you worry that your father will not approve."

Cain looked away. "Yes."

He could feel the entity studying him, and Cain wondered the odds of this happenstance.

"Come down to the water brook on the western side of the valley by tomorrow at dawn. You will find what you are looking for there," the entity told him. "It would be wise for you to begin your journey there as soon as possible. As I am sure you know, that is an entire day's walk."

"And what will be there when I arrive?" Cain heard himself ask.

Despite not being able to see the entity's face, Cain could have sworn he "felt" him smile.

"You will see."

"Why are you doing this?" Cain asked.

"I've watched you, Cain. I've protected you even when you didn't know I was there…"

"But why?" Cain pressed, stepping closer.

"I guess you can say, you are like a son to me." And with that, the entity disappeared.

Cain yelped in surprise, jumping back, unsure of what to make of what just happened. A slight breeze rustled the foliage behind him, and he spun around quickly, thinking that the entity had reappeared.

He had not.

Come down to the water brook on the western side of the valley by tomorrow at dawn. You will find what you are looking for there, he heard the entity's voice whisper in his mind. The decision to go was a simple one, being that he had nothing to lose and everything to gain. If his Offering was not enough for his father and The One on High, he had planned on leaving. There would be no point in sticking around and enduring his father's disapproval while Able reaped the benefits of their father's love.

But what if nothing awaited him at the water brook and his trip was in vain?

There was only one way to find out.

Gathering up his pride, Cain turned around and continued his journey towards the camp site where his family slept. He had less than a couple of hours to prepare for the hunt. The only thing he silently hoped for was that Adam would be pleased with what he brought home, and maybe, just maybe, he would feel like he belonged.

Chapter Four

"Where are you going?" Abel's voice interrupted Cain's thoughts as he began to head towards the clearing.

Cain tried his best to ignore his brother's pestering, but as always, Abel had to force him to acknowledge his presence.

"I'm going off to hunt," Cain replied flatly as he wrapped up the remaining dried goat meat and papaya fruit into a cloth.

"But the sun hasn't risen," Abel continued. "You can't hunt in the dark."

"Why are you up, brother?" Cain sighed. "Go back to bed,"

"I heard you coming." Abel shrugged. "I was worried when you didn't come back. Father said to just give you some space."

"Of course, he would," Cain mumbled as he reached for his hunting knife that he made from granite stone and old bark. He strapped the weapon to his ankle before reaching for his spear.

"Where are you going?" Abel repeated, watching his brother.

"To hunt."

"Let me come with you. It is dangerous to hunt alone," Abel pleaded.

"I've hunted alone plenty of times, Abel," Cain stated firmly. "Why would it be any different?"

"Because," Abel began. "Father warned us of an entity that roams about the earth- The Banished One."

Cain paused. Could that have been…?

"I am certain the Archangels will deal with him," Cain said quickly as he walked past his brother.

"Why must you always be so difficult?" Abel shouted.

Cain turned around to meet the same face who shared features very similar to his own. Rich dark skin on a handsomely chiseled face. Somber eyes, full lips, and a head full of hair that Abel refused to tame or loc. Abel, however, looked more like Adam than Cain did. No one spoke of it, but the question still burned in Adam's eyes every time he looked at Cain. He sensed it. His mother smiled and pretended like she knew not of what the problem was. But Cain knew she knew. Something had been amiss since the moment of his birth and throughout his life. Adam's hard stare followed him. The unspoken question seemed silly. After all, Adam was the first human. The first man to spring forth from the dust, a perfect combination of flesh and spirit. Eve had been molded from his rib, the first Wombman. There could not possibly have been another capable of siring. Could it?

Cain brushed off the thought and returned his focus to his brother. "Will you be quiet? Now I'm going. End of story. You collect berries and carrots. I actually have to kill something, which is beyond your understanding, brother." Cain then brushed past his brother without another word.

"Be safe brother," Cain heard Abel whisper into the night.

"Always."

***

Just as the entity had said, the trek to the west side of the valley-by the water brook took an entire day. Cain's body riddled with exhaustion as he approached the bubbling creek. He knew this area, having hunted many a time there, following the trail of the creek until it intertwined with the river that flowed towards the ocean.

His feet begged for him to rest, but he would not stop until he reached his destination. The dried goat meat and papaya fruit had long been devoured. And just as he came a few hundred yards from the rushing water, there it was: the largest bull he had ever laid eyes upon. Magnificent horns protruded in a glorious challenge from the animal's head. Large hooves stomped repeatedly on the grass, a beautiful display of his aggression. He had a shiny black coat that shone brightly under the light of the sun.

Cain gripped his spear tightly and slowly placed his knapsack on the ground. The animal snorted, and began scratching the ground with his hooves, preparing to charge. *This is it,* Cain thought excitedly. *This is what was waiting for me here! Father would surely be pleased.* The animal snorted again and bucked before charging in his direction.

Cain swiftly tumbled to the side, barely missing the bull's horn to his face. The bull skidded to a stop, spun around, and charged again. This time, Cain was ready for the beast. He quickly ducked low as the animal charged and used his hunting knife to slice through the bull's back ankle. The animal screeched in pain, but did a U-turn, focusing his hatred on Cain. The animal missed, and Cain used this as his opportunity to strike the final blow. He plunged his spear straight through its heart. The bull stopped screaming,

[19]

and finally collapsed in a heap. Blood spurted from the chest wound, seeping out onto the grass, staining it.

Breathing heavily, Cain plopped down next to the bull, pulling his knees up to his chest. The morning rays suddenly felt good on his skin. The icy chill that followed him melted away. He'd done it. Thanks to the entity's promise.

Could that have been The Banished One? Cain thought as he studied the bull. The majesty of the animal was striking. Never had he in all his years as a hunter seen something like this. Where had this bull come from?

He didn't yet know that this would be exactly the same question Adam would ask.

***

"That is some bull," Adam stated blandly, suspicion written all over face. "Where did you find it?"

"On the west end, by the creek," Cain said as he continued to drag the dead animal towards the nearly constructed pyre. "It was a blessing."

"Hm," Adam said, still staring at the bull. "Indeed, it was."

"That is some bull!" Luluwa exclaimed from behind. "Where did you find it?"

Her smile was as radiant as the sun. Cain quickly turned away when he noticed his father's disapproving glare, but as she approached, he wondered why Adam rejected the idea of Luluwa being his bride.

"You are going to bring good fortune to this family," Luluwa chirped. "Mother! Come look!"

Eve emerged from the makeshift hut with baby Aklia in her arms. Her rich dark skin glistened underneath the bright light. She wore her locks piled high above her head, after having decorated the ends of a few stray locks with seashells they had gathered many moons ago.

"Oh my!" Eve gasped as her gaze shifted from the bull to her son. "You have proven yourself to be quite the skilled hunter. I am so proud of you!"

His mother's demonstration of pride made Cain's heart swell. His mother had always been good to him. She loved him, and on days when Adam was harder on him that usual, she always gave him a little extra dose of love. Adam, however, kept his eyes focused on the dead bull, his mouth held tightly together. "Where is my brother?" Cain asked his mother who still looked at him with pride.

"He is out preparing for the Offering, as you should be," Adam growled as he stalked off. "I will finish building the pyre."

Cain felt his heart begin to race as pent up anger threatened to spill out into the open. Clenching his fist, he forced himself to summon calm. "Why does he hate me so?" He demanded of his mother, who clung Aklia tightly against her chest.

Luluwa shared and uneasy glance with their mother, and without a word, offered to take her baby sister to give the two of them time to speak.

"Adam loves you," Eve began softly, her eyes pleading with him to just let the situation go.

"Mother, I am going to have respectfully request that you do not lie to me," Cain gritted through his teeth. "What have I done other than be born to deserve the ire of Adam?"

"You have done nothing wrong, my son," Eve said as tears blurred her vision. Cain's heart hurt to see his mother's tears fall like lost diamonds cast from the sky.

"Then tell me why he treats me like an outcast?" Cain continued, wiping away a stray tear from his face. "Tell me. I have done everything this man has demanded of me and still he looks at me as if I plague him with disgust."

"Cain, I—"

"You know what?" Cain spat. "Never mind. I have to prepare the bull before cleansing. It doesn't even matter at this point." Cain looked at the dead bull. Even in death the creature was too beautiful. Too powerful. And, the more the he thought about it, too easy to kill.

The stranger kept his word.

"I will get the herbs that mother and I prepared for you," Luluwa offered as she returned Aklia to Eve.

"Thank you, Luluwa," Cain mumbled, his gaze still focused on the bull.

"No worries, dear brother," she said, placing a gentle hand on his shoulder. "You've done a fine job. I think Adam is so used to you failing that now that you've actually done something right, he doesn't know what to do."

Cain shrugged. "Well, I'm sick of it."

[22]

Luluwa nodded, understanding filling her soft, gray eyes. "We must talk later." Cain nodded before she walked away, leaving him alone with his thoughts.

Let this Offering be a blessed one, he thought to himself. *Please.*

Chapter Five

Cain wished his brother would simply give him space. Even whilst they bathed in the running water that ran closest to Eden, Abel still had to do so in close proximity to Cain. Just because they were twins did not mean that they had to spend every waking moment together. At least, that was how Cain felt.

"You know, brother, the fruits were all ripe for the picking this season," Abel chirped. "I gathered more than enough for The Offering, as well as enough for all of us to enjoy."

"That's wonderful, brother," Cain said dryly as he dipped his body into the cool water. "Truly, it is."

"Where did you find that bull?" Abel asked.

That seemed to the be the question of the day.

"I told you already," Cain said, hoping that his brother would just leave it alone.

"Never seen a bull like that," Abel continued. "At least not around these parts."

"Well, you are not a hunter," Cain snapped. God, why did Abel always have to question everything?

"That may be true, brother," Abel said evenly. "But father is questioning it, too. He is even considering not including the bull for The Offering."

"What?!" Cain roared, splashing over to his brother. "What do you mean he is considering not offering the bull?"

Abel shrugged. "He doesn't trust it and doesn't want to risk offering it only for us to be cursed again."

Cain froze. Icy rage trickled through his veins, stopping and restarting his heart. He glared at his twin, suddenly wishing that he had never been born. Since birth he had to compete with his simpleton brother for simple words of praise. Since birth it seemed as if he was condemned to be the son that Adam never wanted.

"I'm leaving," Cain heard himself announce to his brother. "I cannot do this anymore."

Abel's brows raised high on his head. "What?"

"I'm leaving. Everything I do isn't good enough. Adam—"

"Father," Abel corrected, holding Cain's gaze.

"Adam," Cain continued. "Hates me."

"No, he doesn't," Abel protested.

Cain shook his head and turned around, and then headed towards the grass. Abel reached out and gripped his shoulder, holding him in place.

"Just tell me where you found the bull."

Cain angrily snatched away from his brother. He shoved him hard without thinking. "That's all everyone seems to worry about is where I found the bull! No one seems to appreciate its value or the fact that—"

"Cain!" Adam's hard glare greeted them from the grass. Eve was in the distance, running towards them, screaming Adam's name. Luluwa was not too far behind, with baby Aklia in her arms.

This was it. Cain's fury became redirected at his father. The hard stare from Adam was enough to make his blood boil. Abel sensed the dangerous turn in his brother's mood and tried to hold him back. Adam awaited, his fists clenched, jawline tight and prepared for whatever Cain was willing to deliver.

"Adam!" Eve shouted. "Stop it! Just let him offer the bull! There is nothing wrong with it! He deserves a chance!"

"Why do you hate me so?" Cain challenged as he dragged his brother from the water to face off with his father. "Why? Abel and I shared the same womb, yet you treat me as if I am not of your blood!"

Adam's lip trembled as the cold hard truth spilled from his lips. "You are not of my blood, Cain."

"What do you mean I am not of your blood?" Cain seethed.

"Adam!" Eve shouted.

"War. Hatred. Those things are not of me," Adam stated blandly, meeting Cain's eyes. "From the time of your birth, it was obvious that you took more from your brother than you gave. He was smaller, while you grew stronger."

"I have done nothing but protect not *just* my brother," Cain growled, "But this family. I have provided nothing but the best of meat. Risked my own life for this family!"

"And even so, every action taken has been for yourself," Adam continued.

"Myself?"

"That is why your Offerings were rejected. It had nothing to do with the quality of the animal. It has always been offered with selfish intentions, which is why Abel has always brought blessings upon this family."

[26]

Abel slowly released his hold on his brother. Eve reached out to Cain with open arms to try to bring comfort, but Adam held out his arm to block her. Slow awareness crept into Cain's psyche. Adam did not consider him his blood. Abel would always be the favored son. Adam made it a point to strip everything away from him. As his eyes met the saddened expression of Luluwa, one thing became clear, Adam took from him because he rejected him as his blood.

Blood must be paid for in blood. Cain looked at his brother, whose eyes held instant fear. Everything seemed to happen in slow motion.

Eve screamed. Luluwa covered her mouth, and Adam simply could not move fast enough to stop the inevitable.

Hurt. Despair. Anger. All of that consumed and fueled Cain as he stepped forward and delivered a punch to his brother's head with the brute force of his hammer.

Something snapped.

Blood oozed from Abel's nose and fell to the ground. Cain watched as his brother's lifeless eyes stared back at him. Eve's screams drowned out the sound of his own beating heart.

"What have you done?" Adam whispered as grief took hold of him.

Dark clouds formed against the once serene, blue sky and lightning struck as the ground cried out from its first taste of spilled blood. Blood. So much of it he could drink it, smell it ... bask in it. Darkness ... he was surrounded in darkness ... his parent's grief. His brother—what had he

[27]

done? Nausea and pain like no other claimed and consumed him in a burning fire that sent him to his knees.

"What have you done?"

The booming voice from the sky startled him. It was He Who Made Adam. The Creator.

"Cain, what have you done? The earth cries out to me that the blood of your brother was spilled by your hand. You know not of what thine cast upon thyself ... "

Falling to his knees, Cain looked at his fallen brother. The once green grass that surrounded him turned black as his brother's blood was absorbed into the earth. Cain felt the flesh of his forehead burning with an inscription or mark that would permanently follow him for all eternity. He gingerly touched his forehead where he felt the raised and raw skin of the brand that would forever haunt him with the memory of this moment.

"They will know you by thine thy mark ..." The Creator told him before retreating back into the heavens.

With trembling palms, Cain stood up long after The Creator left, to face a moonless sky. Adam's voice echoed in the backdrop of his mind. But something else happened. The mark that was placed on his forehead melted away, as something, a dark power filled his veins. Like magma, this dark force oozed its way through his veins until it reached his heart, melting away what felt like his humanity. "You are not my son!" He heard Adam shout.

Thunder.

Lightening.

The earth began to tremble beneath him. A pair of soft hands held onto him. He heard Adam shouting at Luluwa to stay back, but she did not. She held on.

Still screaming, he forced himself to his feet again. His throat burned with an unquenchable thirst. Adam's fists pounded against his back, but Cain forced himself away and took off into the darkness.

A fire in his aching belly craved that which did not grow from the land or fall from the skies. He ran until he found himself secluded and surrounded by a family of trees that seemed to extend an endless reach into the heavens. Here, he would beg for forgiveness. Sobbing, he cried out, "I have been forsaken!" The sky had blackened with angry dark clouds, an expression from Mother Nature herself that she too was displeased with his actions. "All I have done! And this is how I am repaid!"

He had no awareness of time when he slipped into unconsciousness. But during those moments, he dreamed of nothing but blood. Rivers of blood. Oceans of blood. The sky rained blood. He came to eventually, still surrounded by total darkness. He sat up quickly, noticing the changes in his body. He could see things with a deeper clarity, like the wood of the tree. He could see the very distinct definition and structure of the bark. He could make out a fly that landed on the leaf of the adjacent branch. Even the translucent design of its wings didn't escape his vision. And then it dawned on him. He was now an outcast. A man without a family. Without a home. His thoughts returned to the very moment he killed his brother. He lost control. He would forever mourn the death of Abel. But now he knew that humans, as they were, could perish. He'd never known that fact until now.

Another question soon plagued him as he paced to and fro'
in the forest. What would happen to his sister Luluwa?
Would Adam punish her for her affections towards him?
She did not deserve the harshness of their father's
punishments, not ever. Suddenly fear for what would befall
Luluwa unnerved him. He could surely kill Adam, but to do
so, would incur the wrath of the One On High.

But there was still time…

Chapter Six

Running, Cain knew exactly where his family would take refuge. He could sense them, but a few miles away. His heightened awareness both terrified and thrilled him at the same time. The sounds of the night creatures nearly deafened him with their calls. With the strength and stealth of a lion, he rushed through the forest with a force he'd never experienced. What was he? And how? What had the Almighty done? Question after question rushed through his mind as he sped through the night.

He returned to the Cave of Treasures, where his family continued to grieve. A trail of smoke emptied from the opening of the cave. He could hear his father's voice. The grief and anger that it carried struck a core within Cain. The urge to creep inside and put an end to Adam grew strong as he approached, until he caught the scent of Luluwa near the cave's entrance. Carefully, he took his time with his approach, not wanting to scare her, or worse, alert Adam of his presence. Wrapped in the skin of a ram, she kept her focus on the dark sky.

"Luluwa," he breathed as he quietly approached.

She whipped her head around quickly in surprise. "Cain?"

"Shh…" He inched his way towards her.

"What are you doing here?" She whispered back. "Father will kill you on sight."

"I know," Cain said once he stood directly in front of her. "But I had to make sure that you are alright."

Luluwa studied him, her body tense. He knew she was afraid, but still she stayed. "You are different," she observed. "Darker."

"Come with me," he heard himself say. "You don't have to stay here. I will protect you."

She looked away and returned her gaze to the sky. "Father has summoned the presence of Archangels. He knows that you are…different."

He paused. The Archangels were involved in this too?

"He wants you executed for taking Abel away from him," she continued. "And mother, well she is devastated."

He swallowed thickly. Pain for what he'd done to his mother and to his brother would indeed haunt him forever.

"And do you want me executed too, Luluwa?" he asked, afraid of her answer.

She looked at him, sadness filling her eyes. "No. I do not. I love you, brother. Always have and always will."

"Then, come with me. Be more than my sister, but my wife, and I promise you that I will spend the rest of my days dedicated to giving you the best life possible."

She held his gaze, those slanted gray eyes of hers more beautiful than any sunset. "If I go with you, the angels will hunt me too."

"I have the power to protect us both," Cain vowed. "Please go with me, Luluwa. Please do not leave me alone."

His words seemed to hit her, better yet strike her, like a tree in a lightning storm. "If you are alone, then I am alone too.

[32]

I will go with you." She stood up and rushed over to him, filling his arms with her warm body.

Luluwa, his sister and his love and the very fabric of what was left of his dark soul, touched his face. Her gray eyes filled with unshed tears. She held his gaze and nodded, and as their parents slept, they stole away into the night.

Cain learned of his new abilities in the darkness. He learned that he possessed nearly no physical limits. Even the animals knew that he was now an apex predator, and for that reason, they remained out of sight. That night, a monster had been born. From the darkness, a byproduct of broken supernatural law, he was something that the earth - though still in its infancy-had never seen before. He carried his sister through miles of thick underbrush, blazing through the forested terrains like a shooting star, settling on a land with rich soil perfect for planting and harvesting, that rested on the southern banks of the Nile River. Exhausted from their night's run, they took shelter underneath a cluster of trees with leaves wide enough to offer supportive roofing. He cradled her next to him, relishing the fact that she had chosen him above their father. She knew that something had changed within him, yet still she trusted him.

But it was on that night that his reality revealed itself.

Unquenchable thirst, insatiable hunger that no fruit or water could ease filled him. The call of Luluwa's heartbeat, the warmth of her body, and the rush of her blood flowing through her veins became all too much of a temptation. That night, Cain lay with his sister-wife Luluwa, whose beauty rivaled her mother Eve, and that bond would be his savior from the scorching thirst that stripped away his sanity. That night, Cain discovered the monster that he truly had become, and that night, he created another one.

Chapter Seven

50 years later

"She still hunts us," Luluwa observed from the protection of the mountaintop dwelling Cain built for them. "I recall a time when she cried for me to carry her when mother would not."

Cain shook his head and continued to keep watch from the bird's eye view they had. "She has reason to. But, still I would hate to be forced to kill another of my own blood."

"Perhaps if we reason with her…" Luluwa stated as she cradled her firstborn, Nunka, close to her bosom.

"There is no reasoning with her," Cain argued. "She is Adam's daughter and the archangels are on her side-."

"We still cannot feed on the humans, then?" Luluwa asked, licking her lips. "Their blood smells divine, even from here."

"Adam's sons are grown now but their families are young," Cain reminded Luluwa with a slight smile. "If we gorge on them, the angels will smite us instantly. We have survived this far because we have not tasted human blood. You were my first and only Luluwa."

"Your blood is sweet my love," Luluwa said with a deep inhale. "But theirs is…"

"Stop, Luluwa," Cain commanded. "We have survived this long without taking a body, and we will continue to do so at least until the human populations have grown in numbers."

Cain's sentence was instantly cut short by a short dagger that barely missed his face. Cain pushed Luluwa and their son out of the way, as he in turn moved with the agility of a feline and leaped from the edge of the mountainside into a free fall.

Midflight, he met his younger sister, Aklia, in a collision that sent both of them into a fight to the death all the way down. She landed several hard punches to his jaw and forehead before they separated, tumbling in different directions in a hard roll. Cain was the first to spring to his feet just before his sister launched another attack.

"Infidel!" she shouted, leaping to her feet. She flung as series of small, handheld silver tipped daggers towards him. They flew like tiny missiles, which he barely missed.

"I do not wish to harm you, sister!" he pleaded, taking refuge behind a tree. "Please!"

"You are no brother of mine!" she spat, lunging for him.

With one swipe, he knocked her into a thicket several yards away. The force of his blow should have killed her, but she was "different" too.

"Father turned you against me. The angels turned you against me," Cain began as he slowly approached. "When I have done nothing to any of you! I've been cursed for a mistake I did not wish to make."

"You are an abomination! Because of you, everything has changed," Aklia screamed as she struggled to get to her feet. "You are the reason mother's tears never dried. You are the reason father's heart has become that of a husk. You are the reason why the angels are suiting up for battle! You are the reason why I must fight!" She unsheathed her sword, a magnificent blade that he had seen only once, and that was in the Garden.

The Cherubim carried something similar to it. The handle was made of pure silver and lined with precious gemstones that he vowed to collect for Luluwa. The light that it emitted was blinding, and Cain raised his arm to cover his face, but disappeared into mist before Aklia could take his head.

"You took Luluwa and condemned her to darkness!" Aklia shouted into the nothingness.

"Dear sister, I will only grant you so much patience," Cain growled, his voice bouncing from the treetops. "There is much you do not understand."

"I understand perfectly! You are a threat to humanity!"

"I have not fed on any human. To do so would mean the end…"

"Come out and fight me!" Aklia screamed in frustration.

"Go home, little sister." Cain sighed. "On this day, I do not wish to kill you."

Cain did not acknowledge her continuous calls to battle. Instead, he left her, battered and bruised from the fall. At some point, when she was stronger and a more seasoned Huntress, they would engage again, and that would be a time when only one of them would walk away. Over the years, he'd tested the limits of his abilities and found none. Luluwa was unable to walk in the sun as he could, which added more to his sorrow. He learned that it was through his bite that he could make more of his kind; and he knew that blood would forever haunt him as a means to his existence. His story began in blood, and therefore he reckoned that would be how it would end.

His sister, Aklia on the other hand, was still human. But she possessed the skillset of Archangel Michael, and the physical strength of a hundred men. She was his match, blow for blow, and before he put an end to her, he needed to know if more like her would come. He needed to know her purpose and how she fit into all of this. What role did any of them play in the master plan orchestrated by The One on High?

He materialized next to Luluwa, who cuddled their son Nunka close to her. The sun was too high in the sky and drained her of her energy, which meant that Cain would have to assume fatherly duties until dusk. He hated what he'd done to her and dreaded to find out more about his "Curse". One thing that he was grateful for was the fact that neither of them appeared to age, and perhaps, they would remain frozen in time for eternity. The problem however, rested with the fact that their son would grow, as would his blood hunger.

And then what would become of them?

Chapter Eight

And so, another hundred years flew by, and with it the human populations had more than quadrupled in numbers. The sons and daughters of Adam had become fruitful, and finally after a century of near starvation, Luluwa, Cain, and their son Nunka could feast on blood. To indulge in the sweet, rich nectar of human life, to taste the pain, the joy and the lusts of humanity, had proven to be more than addictive. It became an obsession.

Just as the humans replenished themselves, Cain and his family gorged. They moved from land to land, following the trails set by Seth-Cain's younger brother- careful to not feed too much, lest they draw angelic attention as humanity was still within the early stages of infancy. However, within their path of destruction, they left behind a legacy of death. Aklia still hunted them just as ferociously as she had in the past and came awfully close to successfully taking Cain's head.

And once upon a time, Cain had almost let her when he realized what he had done.

"Cain." He overheard Luluwa summon him as she released the dead body of Seth's runaway grandson.

He tuned to face her "Yes, Luluwa?"

"What shall we do with this body? I have already snapped his neck so that he does not turn."

"Leave it. I will come back before sunrise and dispose of it."

"Seth will hunt us for this," Luluwa said sadly. "What have we become?"

"Aklia's daughters are strong like their mother," Cain reminded her. "We will keep surviving as we have always done."

"Seth's sons also grow strong and look to Aklia to lead an army," Luluwa whispered.

"It is the price we pay for what we are. Where is Nunka?" Cain asked, searching the surrounding darkness for their son.

Instantly, Cain dematerialized out of the hidden shadows of the jungle in which they hid before he realized he was too late. Nunka, now a fully adult vampire, with all of his father's strengths and none of his mother's weaknesses, stood out in the open. His face was covered in blood as he stared at the young woman off in the distance bathing in the river. His gaze remained fixated on the gorgeous dark skin that blended in with the deep, crystal clear waters.

"Who is she?" Nunka asked.

"That looks like Adrina.Aklia's oldest daughter," Cain stated flatly.

"She is beautiful." Nunka breathed.

"She is dangerous," Cain added. "She is a Huntress like her mother. And she is a thousand times more lethal because I killed her Fath-" A dagger sliced through the air, interrupting Cain's sentence and piercing Nunka's shoulder.

"How dare you watch me while I bathe!" Adinkra cried out, wrapping a goat's skin around her even as she lunged forward.

The woman moved like lightening, and in a flash, Cain snatched his injured son and the two of them deconstructed into mist, disappearing before Adinkra could catch them.

"What were you thinking!" Cain shouted at his son. Luluwa rushed forward to help. But when she noticed the silver dagger still burning a hole through Nunka's shoulder, she hissed.

Nunka collapsed on a pile of leaves, grimacing from the pain. "I just wanted to see who she was! Her beauty is like that of no other!"

"Her beauty is what lured you," Cain growled as he kneeled down next to his son.

"Then make me a bride, then!" Nunka shouted as Cain yanked out the silver dagger.

Luluwa gasped at the request.

"Do you know what such a request requires?" she asked, sharing an uneasy glance with Cain.

"It is not right that I am alone," Nunka groaned. "Father has you, Mother, and what do I have? Human women do not survive long enough."

"I told you to control yourself, son."

"Make me an equal!" Nunka demanded.

The silence that befell them drowned out the white noise of Cain's rage. He understood Nunka's need for companionship. Soon, he was certain that his son would dare to venture off into the world on his own, independent and unrestrained from his parents. Something that Cain also feared would get him killed.

"I will not turn Adrina," Cain growled.

"Then I will find a woman whose beauty rivals that of Adrina," Nunka stammered.

Cain said nothing as he bit into his wrist, opening a vein for his son to feed from.

"You are right, it is not fair that you are alone. That is something that I almost faced myself and had it not been for your mother, I would have had no choice but to face the darkness alone."

Nunka accepted his father's wrist and took in several deep pulls before releasing it. "Thank you, Father."

"You're welcome, son."

Remove this space.

Cain and Luluwa shared another look, worry filled those beautiful gray eyes of hers that reminded him of the very silver that pierced Nunka's shoulder. "Worry not my love," he told her. "This will be the first and only sacrifice we make. Perhaps we find the most wicked of Adam's daughter's that should be a fit to be a bride for Nunka. If we turn one of innocent blood, the angels will surely come for us. We must wait until we find one that calls for darkness."

"And then we make her the nightmare that she dares to dream," Luluwa says with a grin.

Chapter Nine

The screams of the innocent cut through the darkness like a blade as Cain sank his fangs deep into the throat of his young victim. Barely sixteen years of age, he tasted the sweet nectar of her youth through her blood. Luluwa greedily took her wrist and bit down again. The girl went limp and lifeless from the brutality of their collective feeding. Dawn slowly approached, burning away the darkness inch by inch. Luluwa quickly licked away at the wound, savoring the taste of the dead girl's blood before disappearing back to their caved lair. Cain anticipated that Nunka retreated back to the cave to rest after a night of hunting.

He released the girl, apathetically watching her body collapse onto the dry soil with a hard thud. Whispers from beneath the earth's surface called to him, taunting him as they did the night he turned Luluwa into his equal. *Blood drinker*, they called him. *Defiler*, they said.

He reasoned that his guilt was slowly stripping away his sanity, and for he feared that he would soon lose himself in the call of blood. He stared at the lifeless body, remembering the first night after decades of living off of the blood of his wife.

He'd killed Seth's oldest son, Enos. The boy had barely reached the early years of manhood, maintaining a strong resemblance to both his father and Adam. And, perhaps, Cain reasoned, that may have strengthened the urge to kill his nephew.

"Father, even after all this time, you still haunt me," Cain said out loud. No one would hear him, other than the small flock of colorful birds that nested high up in the treetops.

The rage he had always wanted to direct towards his father returned to the surface. But as much as he would have liked to hunt down the very man who not only sired him but brought forth this curse; the angels redirected Adam, Eve, and their young children to higher lands that he could not cross. There they would remain guarded, lest they become foolish like their older children and decide to leave.

"It's been quite some time since we've met like this," came the all too familiar voice that materialized behind him.

Cain quickly turned around to see the silhouette of a massive, winged, human-like figure whose face and physical description was shrouded in absolute darkness. Even with his heightened senses, Cain's eyes strained to see the entity that stood casually before him.

"Please don't tell me that you've forgotten about me," the entity chirped.

Cain looked away. "I have not. I remember you."

"Good. I take it Adam didn't like the bull?"

Cain swallowed thickly, recalling Adam's judgmental and scrutinizing stare upon his return with the bull.

"You are the reason…" Cain whispered, as more memories of that fateful morning after the bull incident stormed his memory.

"I am the reason for many things, Cain," the entity replied evenly.

"The bull," Cain growled. "You knew that bull would cause strife in my family!"

"They were never your family, Cain."

[44]

"They *are my family!*" Cain spat, fangs lengthening to a saber-toothed proportions.

The entity sighed, shaking his head. "There is so much that you do not know. But Adam knows…and perhaps in time, so will you."

Cain snarled and lunged at the entity, who disappeared instantly, dodging Cain's snatch attempt, only to reappear behind him.

"You cannot harm me." The entity chuckled.

Cain released a frustrated growl. "*Who are you?*"

The entity paused, the darkness around him thickening. "I've been around long before the creation of the stars, long before the earth circled the sun for the first time…and you do not even know who I am?"

This time, it was Cain's turn to pause. "No…you were *banished!*"

"I am no longer welcomed in the higher realms," the entity replied coolly. "But here, I can roam about as I please."

Instant recognition filtered into Cain's awareness. All this time, it was none other than the original Fallen.

"I helped you, Cain," the entity stated. "And I will continue to help you."

"Why?" Cain whispered.

"Because you and I share more than just a single commonality of being misunderstood and underappreciated," the being said calmly.

"Because of you," Cain hissed. "I am cursed!"

[45]

"I saved you," the entity continued on. "What would have happened to you would have been far worse than anything that you in your human condition would have never been able to survive."

"Why?"

"Because you are mine!" The sonic wave that emitted from the entity's voice shook the treetops, sending a flock of birds scattering into the air.

"You will rise to a power you would have never dreamed of," the entity continued. "Your name will be branded in the history books as it will be my legacy."

"What are you talking about?" Cain demanded, marching closer to the being.

The entity took a step back, and Cain could sense the smile that spread evenly across his face.

"Ask Eve."

And just as quickly as the entity appeared, he was gone. Cain stared at the spot where the entity once stood, with extended fangs, and sudden awareness.

Ask Eve... the entity's last words replayed in his mind, summoning a fearful dread of what it could have meant. His mother now resided on protected and blessed land – land that he didn't dare cross. His instincts told him upon approach, that his death would be imminent. He knew the angels stood guard, protecting the first woman, the first mother of humanity from all harm.

What sins have you committed, Mother? Cain thought to himself as he turned to walk away. *What have you done?*

Chapter Ten

"You cannot be serious!" Luluwa hissed, springing to her feet.

"Father!" Nunka shouted from behind her. "You know what will happen if you travel there!"

"You cannot leave me alone in this condition!" Luluwa continued. "I believe I am once again with another child!"

Both Cain and Nunka stopped and looked at the distraught Luluwa. Her gray eyes filled with unshed tears. Her beautiful, heart shaped face was slightly more rounded. Cain inhaled deeply. He'd known. In a few months' time, another baby blood drinker would curse this planet. Yes, he would shower it still with all of the love and affection that a doting father would, but deep down, he resented the abnormality of all of this. He loved his wife with his soul. She had always been loyal to him. She had always demonstrated nothing but love to him.

But like him, she was death in the flesh. Preserved in rare beauty wrapped in ebony; eyes like silver fire; hair thick as rope that never ceased to grow from her beautiful scalp; but as lethal as cobra, only ten times deadly. Long gone was the innocent sister he fell in love with. What stood before him was a monster.

And he was the one to blame for it- for all of it.

"I must," Cain insisted, approaching his wife and gently taking her palms into his. "There are answers that I need in order to understand all of this, all of what we are and all of what we may be destined to become."

[47]

"We are what we are!" Nunka argued. "Why do you need answers to questions that we do not need to know?"

Cain looked at his wife, who nodded with understanding. "Because son, I was human before you were born."

Nunka's eyes widened as he stared at his father in disbelief. "No. That cannot be."

"It's true," Luluwa agreed. "As was I."

"Your grandfather is Adam, but it is not Adam I wish to speak with," Cain replied, still holding Luluwa's gaze. "I need to speak with Eve."

Luluwa's gasp filled the cavern. "Adam will never allow you to speak with her."

"I have to try. Besides, she spent plenty of time alone in the Garden before," Cain shrugged. "I am certain that Eve still enjoys bathing in the river alone. I just have to make certain that she is alone."

"Then take me with you," Nunka pleaded.

Cain shook his head. "Stay here with your mother. Aklia still hunts us despite us being separated by entire lands now."

"When are you going?" Luluwa asked.

"I am leaving now," Cain said before placing a gentle kiss on her forehead. "I will return soon."

Cain deconstructed into mist and took to the airwaves. The peaceful stillness of the night put his thoughts at ease. Eve would never venture into the night alone to bathe in the river, and the lands where she and Adam were hidden met right where the Tigris and the Euphrates conjoined and emptied out into the sea. He knew his mother like he knew himself, and a part of him still yearned for her love and warmth. By daybreak, he figured was when he would find her. He knew the angels stood as sentinels to protect the first mother of humanity, and if his life would come to an end upon this lone encounter, then so be it. He had to know the truth.

Even if it killed him.

***

Perhaps it was the slow drain from the sun's rays inflicted on him that forced Cain to return to corporeal form just a few miles south of the lands of which Adam and Eve now resided.

Or maybe it was just plain old nerves that forced him into physical form.

The density of the atmosphere that surrounded him thickened. Instinct screamed for him to turn around and retreat home to his now pregnant wife and son. But the other part of him, the part that still clung to the memories of his human days, needed to know the truth. From the moment of his birth it seemed, Adam hated him. And the all the while his mother acted as if Adam was just as perfect and just as ever. For years, Cain thought his mother was simply fulfilling her role as the humble and dutiful wife that the Creator shaped her to be.

But now he supposed that there was more to it.

He walked quickly across the soft grassy plains, admiring the perfect union between land and sky that stretched on for miles. Memories of his time as a child, playing and running with his brother, while his mother and older sister looked on, haunted him. How he missed those days. For years, he yearned for Abel's annoying but cheerful presence. His younger brother had been the day to his night, the moon to his night sky... The memory of him striking his brother plagued him, torturing him with the endless replaying of the shattered look on Abel's face as life was pulled out of his body.

As he contemplated this even further, he realized that he embodied that of which he had done. Death.

Would his mother still look at him as her son, or would the angels strike him down before he even had the chance to speak with her?

The sound of far off laughter caught his attention.

Children.

There were children.

The sloshes and splashes in the water gave Cain pause. He had hoped to speak with Eve alone.

More laughter. More splashes.

And then came Eve's voice. He would recognize that soft, melodious tone of hers anywhere in the world.

And how much he missed her.

"Come on, children," she cooed.

"But, Mother," came the small voice of a little girl. "The water tickles as we play! We must stay longer!"

"No," Eve said. "You have been here long enough." Eve said sternly. "We must go."

"Mother," came the voice of the older boy. "Who is that man off in the distance? Are we expecting visitors?"

Cain stopped several yards away from them. Eve stood up quickly, gathering her robing as she looked back at him. Their eyes met and instant knowing awakened within her. He watched her, waiting for her to do perhaps what Adam instructed her to do after their last goodbye, which was run.

But, she didn't.

She stood frozen by the bank of the river, surrounded by all four of her children, with unshed tears glistening in her eyes.

"Cain?" she whispered.

Her voice struck him like lightening. He remembered crawling into her lap as a child, and her rocking him to sleep after hours of crying because of Adam's belittling. Her voice had always soothed him.

"Mother..."

"Mother, who is that?" the oldest boy asked.

Eve looked down at her young son and gave him a reassuring smile. "Take your siblings and go back to the hut. I will be there shortly."

The boy looked at his mother, and then at Cain curiously, before collecting his siblings. They reluctantly followed their mother's instructions, periodically looking back at her until they disappeared into the thicket of bushes.

Cain slowly approached Eve, who stood with her hands hanging loosely at her sides, and tears sliding down her cheeks. His mother's tears were like precious gems that should never be wasted to water the ground. Rain was for the earth. Her tears were not. She still looked beautiful, with her rich dark skin, full lips, and gray eyes. The same eyes that stared back at him every night through Luluwa.

"My son…" Eve whispered as she reached up to touch his face.

"Mother, I've missed you," Cain said softly.

"You are different," she commented, looking up at him.

"I am," Cain replied evenly.

'The Curse…"

"Yes…."

Eve pulled away as another tear rolled down her cheek. "You must leave now, Cain," Even began, fighting back more tears. "You are within the borders of protected land."

Cain shrugged. "I came to ask you something."

Eve wiped her face and a crystal tear dripped from her palms. "What is it that you ask?"

Cain studied his mother silently, hoping that she would be truthful, because regardless of whatever truth she revealed, he would still hold her in his heart as he always did.

Exhaustion began to claim him, and the air around him slowly became difficult for him to breathe. Beads of sweat formed at his brow. He realized then that his time with his mother was limited.

"Cain, you have to leave. This land is encased with silver – something the angels said would be a weapon against you. The soil you stand on was designed to—"

"What happened in The Garden?" Cain spat quickly.

His mother stared at him blankly. "You know what happened son."

"I know what I was told. Serpent tempts Eve with forbidden fruit. Eve accepts and then tempts Adam with the same fruit—"

"What exactly do you want to know?" Eve demanded, placing both hands on her hips.

"What happened between you and the serpent?" Cain asked. The ground suddenly seemed so far away. The world around him began to spin.

"Eve!"

Both turned in the direction of Adam's voice. Cain's incisors lengthened at the mere sound of his father's voice.

"Coming!" Eve shouted back. Her gaze nervously returned to Cain, who had nearly bulked in size, looking every bit of a nightmare that he knew he could be.

"I have to go!" Eve pleaded to him. "If Adam sees us here, he will assuredly kill you!"

"I need to know, Mother," Cain growled. "Tell me and I promise you that I will never bother you with my presence again."

Eve swallowed thickly. Adam called out to her again, sounding closer than he was before. "I was tempted by the Serpent to eat the fruit," she rattled off quickly. "Once I ate

[53]

the fruit, he tempted me again with pleasures of the flesh that I had not known of and didn't dare speak of."

"What do you mean 'pleasures of the flesh'?" Cain hissed as the awareness dawned on him.

"My body became one with his…" Eve whispered as new tears formed in her eyes.

"And then you went home to Adam."

"I did as The Fallen One instructed so that Adam would not petition the angels to have me exterminated," she said.

"Eve!"

"I said I am coming!" Eve huffed.

"So I am not Adam's son?" Cain asked, feeling what was left of his dark heart shatter to a million pieces. A part of him had known something had been amiss with Adam. But now, everything made sense.

"No. Adam knew this and nearly killed me after you were born. But Gabriel told him not to do so, and that my punishment would be to live with the knowledge of my sin."

"I am everything that I am because of you," Cain said pointedly. "I was rejected by both my father and the Creator because of something you did…"

"And for that, I am so sorry my, son."

"I. Am.. Not. Your. Son." Cain growled. "I am *not* your son!"

A silver tipped arrow whizz past his shoulders, barely grazing the skin. Cain spun around quickly to find his sister

Aklia and her daughter Adinkra running at full speed, surrounded by several golden orbs. He knew that the battle would soon be lost if he did not retreat.

"Because of your indiscretions, you have damned this earth with something that even the angels wish not to see," he began as he deconstructed into mist. "Our tie as mother and son has been broken and as punishment..." He hesitated as another speeding arrow flew past him. "I will bring ruin to all the Sons of Adam. You will be remembered as the *mother* of the living curse rather than the mother of creation itself. And there will be nothing you can do but to watch the earth bleed red."

Her wails followed him as he disappeared into the ethers. Aklia's battle cry still echoed in his ears as he took flight. The image of his mother, the first woman to ever walk the earth, broken and defeated, was something that he would never forget.

Part II

Rebirth and Blood

Chapter Eleven

Several centuries passed and the human population multiplied nearly tenfold. News of Adam's death spread through the network of tribal humans that remained under the protection and leadership of Aklia. *Finally*, Cain thought to himself as he stared up at the moonless night sky. But his mother had passed just a few years before, and that was an ache that he would never be able to get rid of. So many things had transpired between them. Unspeakable truths that even at this point in his life, he refused to revisit.

The single-story dwelling made of mud and stone he shared with his pregnant wife Luluwa, their three growing fledglings, Tati, Tyre, and Eliana, had been built by the hands of humans he enlisted for help. Nunka had finally found his own bride, a beautiful dark-skinned daughter of a chief from the northern tribe of Seth. She was as vicious as Nunka before being turned- so much so- that she had been cast out by her own people. By the time Nunka had discovered her, she had already killed several members of her tribe, claiming that the pagan goddess of fire ordered their execution. But her father had known the truth about his blood thirsty daughter. Unwilling to kill her, putting an end to her psychopathic and sadistic behavior, he decided to cast her out into the wilderness.

And that was how Nunka found her.

And together, the two of them rained a vengeful bloodshed upon that very village when she had awakened to her thirst.

At first, Cain wanted to kill her, believing that her existence would bring attention to Aklia and her daughters. And it did. However, in a surprise attack orchestrated by Nunka and his wife, Naima, the two of them successfully killed

Aklia's oldest and strongest daughter, Adinkra. And in a sadistic ploy to taunt Aklia, they left Adinkra's broken, bloodied body out in the open, hanging by her neck in a treetop clearing.

Aklia's screams could be heard for miles.

However, their victory was short lived. Neither would have known that a bite inflicted upon Aklia's daughter would have resulted in both Nunka and Naima's longsuffering internally. It was then that Cain discovered that his sister and her daughters were something else too. Something designed to combat his family. Their blood proved toxic to blood drinkers, causing temporary blindness, pain, and even their healing abilities stripped from them. Cain and Luluwa assisted with providing both of them with enough blood to keep them alive. Once they were strong enough to be moved, Cain enlisted the aid of human helpers to assist with the construction of their separate homes.

Nunka's abode was positioned over the edge of a cliff less than a mile away, looking downward over a mountain of jagged rocks and a guaranteed death for the unlucky human who dared to venture into Nunka's territory. They now knew and understood the importance of Cain's rules regarding secrecy. All of them were being hunted and would forever be hunted, until each one had been taken down.

Cain studied his pregnant wife, delighted that once again, another member of his kind would be born and not bitten. He wondered if Nunka would be able to expand their legacy with his wife, but only time would tell. His three younger children were nearing the ages of adolescence and like Nunka, despite being blood drinkers, could survive on food. Luluwa and Naima needed blood and blood alone.

Luluwa still prepared meals as she did when she was human and caring for her family as she learned from her mother, Eve. But when darkness fell, she was no longer Luluwa, the doting wife and mother of his children. She became a Huntress, a predator…something that he found both beautiful and terrifying at the same time. The duality of the mother and monster that resided in her was fascinating and something to be studied. As the days drew nearer for the birth of the newest addition to his family, he began to do what any loving, considerate husband would do for his wife, bring food home.

She rested peacefully within the dirt hole that he carefully dug just a few feet into the ground, long enough to accommodate her 5'6'' height, and wide enough for her to shift and change positions should she need it. He lined it with blankets made of the skin of goat and ram for her comfort. Some days, their children would join her as she slept, as they preferred the night anyways. But now they waited for her to awaken from her rest, and the three opted to skip and run around outside as normal children would.

Yet, it was just their luck that a wanderer found his way near their home, unaware of the danger.

Cain quickly stood up from the corner he rested in. "Tati! Tyre! Eliana!" he shouted, moving at light speed to retrieve them, only to discover that they were nowhere to be found. Cursing, he rounded their home, listening for them.

His children were also predators.

A loud scream echoed not far off in the distance of the trees.

With a sigh, Cain materialized from inside the dwelling to where the gurgling sounds of a man on his last breath struggled to pull away from the three fledgling vampires that fed on him.

"Tati! Tyre!" Eliana!" Cain called out to them again, this time capturing their attention.

Savages. His children were savages. They looked up at him, each kneeled from different positions surrounding the dead body, with blood and flesh dripping from their exposed fangs. Tati and Tyre, the twins, each chewed away the side of the poor man's neck, while Eliana worked at his thigh.

"Get away from him!" Cain shouted as he approached the body. "What are you doing?"

Tati and Tyre glanced at one another and slowly rose to their feet. On the other hand, Eliana remained on her knees, still leaning over the man like a vulture protecting her prize.

"We were hungry," Eliana stated evenly. "And he is food."

Cain studied the youngest of the bunch, unsure of how to approach the subject matter at hand. What she said was indeed true, but he could not allow them to remain undisciplined. There needed to be a balance, lest the archangels or his sister decided to come for them.

"Eliana," Cain began carefully, still focused on her. "That may be true, but were you not listening when I explained to all of you, despite being the hunters, we are also the hunted?"

Eliana's eyes slowly normalized from blood red to the soft brown that seemed to always melt his heart. "But Papa," she pleaded, pushing herself away from the body. "His blood, it called to us."

"As blood will always do, for our kind," Cain replied, moving his attention from Eliana to the twins. "But you all must be careful. Humans are a very delicate population, and it is true that individually, they stand no chance against us, in greater numbers, they are a danger."

"Then, we should bleed them out one by one," Eliana declared, catching a frown from her sister, Tati.

"No, Eliana." Cain chuckled. "Then what will we do for food if we bleed them out? In a few short years, we could easily destroy humanity, and then what? Your mother and I nearly starved in the beginning."

Tati stuck her tongue out at Eliana, who sneered back at her. "So, what will we do with him?"

Cain exhaled sharply as he examined the body. His children had done quite the job on the poor wanderer. Had he been lost? Did he have a family that would without a doubt come for him? The poor soul's jaw line and jugular had been ripped out. Tati's work was evidenced by the serrated gash that extended from the man's jaw to his shoulder, all the way through to the bone.

"We are going to have burn the body, as usual," Cain said finally. "But not here."

"Let us come with you," Tyre said, licking around the edges of his mouth. "At some point, we will have to know how to do this on our own."

Instead of children who played with toys made of cloth and wood, his children, in the five years since each of their births, had perfected the art of being a predator. They were smarter, faster, and stronger than human children and most adults. They laughed when a victim begged for mercy.

His children were monsters.

But he loved them anyways.

"Grab his feet, Tyre," Cain instructed, as he grabbed the dead man by what was left of his neck.

Tyre did as instructed as Eliana and Tati hung back, waiting for their father's instructions. Cain quickly glanced at them with playful merriment in his eyes. "Oh, and one more thing." Cain smiled. "Try to keep up."

Cain took off running while Tyre still held onto the man's feet and laughed.

"Hey!" Eliana shouted, racing off after them with Tati behind her. "Wait for us!"

Chapter Twelve

"Father," Eliana began as they sat gathered around the small fire Cain made for them. Luluwa sat snuggled close to Cain, who rubbed her pregnant belly.

"Yes, Lily," Cain said, looking in her direction. Lily was the endearing name he sometimes used for Eliana. He affectionately kissed Luluwa's hand, while still massaging her growing belly.

"There is a boy in the east village," she said evenly. Tati covered her mouth and giggled.

"What boy?" Cain demanded, growing concerned. "A human?"

"Yes," Eliana announced, straightening her shoulders. At ten years old, Eliana appeared just as old as her twin siblings, Tati and Tyre, who were nearing the age of fourteen. But all three of them were physically equal to a young adult. Her long, thick hair had been sectioned off into small braids that covered her entire head and extended to well below her waist. She had her mother's eyes and smile but stood closer to Cain six-foot four height. She was not as shapely as Tati, possessing instead, a long, slender build.

"Who is this boy?" Cain frowned.

"His name is Ramand," Eliana continued. "I met him once by the river."

"And you have been spying on him and his family since," Cain grumbled. "I know."

"Eliana," Luluwa began gently. "What do you want with this boy?"

"She wants to turn him," Tyre declared with a laugh. "She thinks that he will accept the fact that she drinks blood and probably would feed on his next of kin if she had to!"

"Tyre!" Cain snapped. "That is enough!"

Eliana got up from where she sat and in a flash of movement, leaped over the fire, and punched Tyre in the face, knocking him backwards. He hissed, baring his fangs, but did not dare meet her challenge.

"Eliana! Sit. Down," Cain barked, glaring at both of them. "Both of you."

Eliana glared at her brother a few seconds longer before turning around to adhere to her father's command. Tyre brushed himself off and returned to his position next to his sister, Tati. Lulwa offered Cain a worried look.

"I do not want to feed off of him," Eliana confessed. "I do not wish to harm his family."

"How old is this boy?" Cain asked.

"He is nearing the age of a man. His mother wants him to find a bride," Eliana stated proudly. "I overheard her tell him that the other night."

"And you," Cain began carefully. "Want to be his wife?"

"Yes," Eliana said, looking her father in the eyes.

"Eliana." Cain sighed, gently moving away from his wife and folding his hands in his lap. "We are not like them."

"But we can blend in," Eliana contested. "I can blend in. They will never know what I am – what we are."

"How? What happens at the first scent of blood?" Cain asked. "You and your siblings have yet to summon enough control even for a tiny scrape."

"I can practice!"

"And what about the fact that we do not age as they do? Hm? Tell me, as your husband changes with time, you will remain forever young. How could you hide that?"

Cain's question left the group in an ocean of silence so deep, he looked to his own sorrow for oxygen. How cruel his life was that his family now had to suffer the other side of the curse that he dared not discuss? He had always feared that his children would fall in love with humans only to find themselves rejected by them or worse, hunted.

"He will love me as I am," Eliana said sharply. "He will accept me and then, once our children are born, he can become like me."

Tyre barked out a hard laugh. "You really think that Ramand, a family who herds sheep and goats and prays to the moon for protection will want someone like you as part of their family? They cower at their own shadows!"

"Tyre!" Cain yelled. "Enough!"

"You stupid simpleton," Eliana hissed. "You are just mad that the only female that would have you is the goat that you mount when—"

"Eliana! Tyre! Be quiet!" Cain's bellow echoed into the clearing, silencing the two would be combatants, but was a far cry from diffusing the tension that brewed between them.

Cain sucked in several deep breaths, unsure of who was more worthy of his fury. "Tyre, leave. But do not hunt anywhere within a five-mile radius of this perimeter."

Tyre glanced at his twin Tati, who shrugged and looked away before hopping on his feet. "Fine."

"And, Tyre," Cain continued, glaring at his son whose fangs slowly came into view. "Do not go anywhere near that family. Am I clear?"

Eliana's frown deepened at the mere reference to the family she wished to protect. Cain caught the quick glimmer of worry in her eyes when she looked at her brother. Both of them knew what Tyre was capable of.

"Yes, Father. I will not harm that goat herding, shadow fearing family," Tyre mumbled as he turned to leave.

"Good."

Tyre dematerialized into the ether, leaving Cain and Eliana to face off while Luluwa and Tati watched.

"Eliana," Cain said, struggling to maintain calmness as he looked at his stubborn daughter. "Humanity is not something you or your siblings were born with. You came into this world as you are, a predator. Your impulses, what is natural to you, your mores, the way that you process your environment...Death has an entirely different meaning to you than it does to humans. I was human once, or at least for a time, I believed that I was. And because of this, I am asking you to think about this: if you care about this boy and his family like you say you do, you will leave them alone."

"But I can protect them," Eliana argued. "I can keep them safe."

"Eliana, are you aware of what happens when a human is bitten by one of us?" Cain asked. "Nunka, your foolish brother and his even more foolish wife have been quite careless with the disposing of the bodies when they are done, and as a result, we are now an infection to the humans."

"I have killed quite a few of those things," Eliana hissed. "Like I said, I can protect them."

"And what will protect them from you?"

Eliana paused, but despite the question, she remained undeterred. "I will prove to you that I can control my thirst. I will master it. We can eat human food. I will not partake of human blood."

Cain raised an eyebrow at his daughter, and for the first time in his entire existence, he was speechless. Out of his four children, Tyre and Eliana were the most savage. Nunka had engaged in his fair share of sadistic bloodshed, preferring to taunt his victims until nothing but terror spiked their blood. However, Eliana, had been the one that brought him the most concern.

From the moment she could walk, she preferred blood over food. She hunted animals at first for sport, often crushing their skulls in her tiny hands as enjoyment. She took pleasure on her first hunt, when she took down a man at least three times her size and equally as lethal. The man fought hard against Cain, successfully landing a few blows of his own. But Eliana had melted into the shadows and launched a carefully played out attack on the man from behind. Cain could never forget the horror and the awe of witnessing Eliana expertly yank the man's spine straight of out of his back. The man's screams still echoed in the back of his mind as he watched Eliana excuse herself without another word.

The most violent of his brood wanted to change with the hope of being loved and accepted into a world that would only view them with fear. His sister and her offspring hunted them. Humans were becoming wiser and learned new methods of protection. Humans had quickly learned that monsters did exist and there were some things that might be worse than the devil.

As she gazed up at the stars before shifting into mist and he knew exactly where she'd gone.

"Tati," Cain said after a beat, still looking in the direction that Eliana had gone. "Watch over your brother. Make sure he doesn't do anything regrettable."

"Yes Father," Tati replied, springing to her feet.

Once Cain and Luluwa were alone, he gently picked up her hand and held it in his. Her gaze met his. She knew without him telling her that his worry for Eliana was deeper than the darkest trench in the sea. For the first time, the monster – his precious little monster, Eliana- became human, and for that, Cain worried that that alone would kill her.

"Do you think Tati can get to Tyre before he does what I hope he does not?" Luluwa asked.

"I will not have infighting between my children," Cain stated firmly. "He knows what not to do. He has been warned repeatedly to not push Eliana over the edge."

"He loves Eliana's darkness just as much as he loves blood," Luluwa whispered. "Although we are what we are, tempering our urges is what separates us from the damned." Her gray eyes filled with crystal clear tears. "Or are we really truly damned?"

Her question gave him pause. Memories of life when he was but a boy and believed to be Adam's son flooded his vision. The night of his transformation, the spilling of Abel's blood, his own thirst for blood and the last few hundred years of fighting his own sister and her children, running and hiding, all in the name of survival, made everything clear.

"No," he said softly. "We are much more than that…So much more."

Chapter Thirteen

There was absolutely nothing he could do as he looked down at the disemboweled remains of Ramand and the drained corpses of his family. Nothing. Tyre had been given one direct order and still he disobeyed. Eliana's eyes blackened with rage, her silence a guarantee of a death well deserved for her brother. Her hands tightened into clenched fists; her nails dug so deep into her palms that blood dripped onto the mud. Luluwa's eyes were filled with sorrow as she looked at the mess that Tyre made of the bodies. He even slaughtered most of the sheep and goats, and by morning, the sun revealed a nightmarish result of Tyre's violence.

Nunka remained as stoic as ever, expressionless and emotionally void, although Cain knew deep down that Nunka felt that Tyre had gone entirely too far. This was not the family he wanted to create.

"I am so sorry, Lily," Luluwa said softly to her daughter, who stared at what was left of Ramand.

"Tati helped him," Eliana growled. "She *always* helps him because that is what twins do."

"Nunka and I are going to find them," Cain promised, his heart breaking and filling with rage at the same time.

"*And do what exactly?*" Eliana snapped. "Nothing. Just as you have always done. All Tyre does is destroy and kill. You always warned us, you gave us rules to live by, and what does Tyre do? Breaks them. Each and every rule, every boundary set. He did this on purpose! Everything I *love*, he makes it a point to take from me!"

"At the end of the day, Lily," Cain heard himself say. "We are a family."

"This is not family," Eliana croaked as tears cascaded down her face. "I have seen family. This—" she said pointing at Ramand and his father's bodies. "Was family. We are not family. Tyre does what Tyre wants regardless of who he hurts while you stand back and do nothing!"

Cain approached his daughter, desperate to take her into his arms and take away her pain. "Lily, I will find Tati and Tyre and punish them for what they've done. This was treason."

Eliana pushed him away as more tears fell from her eyes. She looked angrily at Luluwa, who stood near Nunka, looking on helplessly, and then at Cain. "This goes beyond treason Father," she said, as she closed her eyes. "I am going to hunt them down to the ends of the earth, even if I have to uproot them from the very bowels of the pit if they think hiding there will save them. Tyre will pay for what he's done, and when I am done with him, Tati will suffer as well."

"Eliana!" Cain reached out to grab her, but she instantly became mist and disappeared into the ether. "Eliana! Eliana!"

There was no response. A soft breeze carried the traces of her scent away with it, leaving behind the remains of the night's horrors. Off in the distance, a scavenger dog cried out to its pack. The heat of the sun rising in the distance reminded him that it was imperative that his wife retreat to the safety of their lair.

"Nunka, see to it that your mother arrives home safely, and please keep watch over her. I will return soon."

"Where are you going?" Luluwa asked. "Eliana is just upset. She would never harm her brother, regardless of what he does."

"Luluwa, my love, if you believe that, then I am afraid you do not know Eliana as well as you think. I have to get to Tyre and Tati before she does, so at least I can stop her from killing them."

"But Father, Tyre crossed a line," Nunka pleaded. "Even I would have executed him for the crime he committed."

"I will not have my children killing each other! I just will not have it!" And with that, Cain disappeared, instantly becoming one with the molecules and using his senses to locate his son.

As he sped through the airwaves, he grew to understand Eliana's perspective. She was born into a family of blood drinkers. She fed off of humanity, but a part of her craved more than just the blood. She wanted to be a part of the human collective, even if only for a little while. She wanted a little light considering the fact that she was surrounded by so much darkness.

And to think that he once craved the same thing.

***

The sun crested just above the horizon as Cain materialized onto the sandy banks several miles west of where he and his family rested. Before he took solid form, the blood that tainted the air was on his pallet. He cringed at the sight of what Tyre left behind.

Complete and total madness was what it was.

Tati's scent still clung to the air like the skin of his sheep that Luluwa hung on the wall. The small village that just hours before was filled with life, love, and expectation of tomorrow, wiped out. Gone. Just like Ramand's. He'd always wondered which one of his children would go insane with blood lust, and a part of him believed it would be Eliana. But Eliana had found humanity through the love of a boy she wished to marry.

His gums thickened as his fangs lengthened. So much blood. The temptation to feed from the dead like carrion struck him with a force he had never known, and he summoned with all of his will the strength to suppress the urge. But a woman lied before him, bare breasted, her thighs twisted at an impossible angle, and her neck, chewed through the bone. Her eyes closed, but her mouth was still opened in silent horror. A child, perhaps no older than eight, lie motionless on the side of a small tree. A man's arm greeted him as he took a step, followed by his torso. Entrails were pulled and stretched out to line the entrance of the mud dwelling. More blood.

Cain slowly walked through the carnage, studying the extent of his son's murderous rampage. Aklia would surely come to avenge these humans. Even on his worst night, Cain would have never resorted to this level of violence and savagery. He taught them how to make clean kills. He taught them when to feed and the importance of self-control. But here he stood, staring at the glossy eyes of a dead man whose head had been separated from his body. He would have to burn this awful memory before humans flocked over to investigate.

A younger female, just a few feet away from him, struggled to push herself up by the small fire that still burned. Her dark hair covered her face, most of it sticking to her with her own blood. Massive bite wounds covered the back of her neck, her arms, and her sides.

Cain shook his head as he continued to approach.

He remembered the first time he realized he had the power to turn a human. He had long believed Luluwa to be a flux or better yet the result of their mated bond. It was one of Seth's sons. Cain had left the body, believing it to be dead. He buried it underneath a small cluster of Mangroves only to discover it walking along the sides of the river sometime later. The boy, somehow reanimated and with a greater thirst for blood than his own, stumbled through the darkness, confused as to what he had become. Cain recalled studying him to see what the boy would do, and surely enough, he homed on to his homeland and went there. Had Cain not intervened, the boy would have bled his own sister dry.

Cain ripped his head off his shoulders that night, hoping that that would be enough to put him down. And it worked.

This morning, it would be the same.

Chapter Fourteen

Aklia and her daughter Lana should their heads in disbelief as they stumbled upon yet another small village, slaughtered. Aklia's surviving daughters, Lana, Amaya, Moon, and her sons Yam and Elan spread out, gasping in the horror that waited for them. Sheathing her sword, Aklia kneeled down to take in another look at the mutilated body of an older woman. Angry tears filled her eyes as she wanted so desperately to plunge her blade into the chest of her brother and every single blood drinker that he created. Cain's birth had become nothing more than a curse upon this planet. Everything she loved dearly had been either stripped away or broken down because of fear -fear of Cain, and all that he would do.

Before her death, Eve barely slept through the nights now that Adam had perished. She still mourned the loss of both of her sons: one to darkness and one to death. She mourned the losses of more of her family as their bloodline expanded when Seth and Aklia had their children. Cain picked them off one by one, until both Adam and Eve had no choice but to move to blessed lands provided to them by the angels themselves to ensure humanity's survival.

And as humanity grew, so did Cain's thirst for blood.

But the air held an entirely different signature. It revealed the presence of Cain's twins, Tati and Tyre, and the desire to put an end to their miserably long existences pooled to the surface of her skin. The neighboring tribes were now frightened-terrified to venture out past their own huts because of the rumors of the blood gods.

There were no blood gods. Only Cain and his abominations of offspring.

"These are fresh kills," she announced. "They are close, perhaps in a cave nearby resting. We will use daylight as our cover. Remember everything I've taught you."

"Yes, Mother," the group murmured.

They all spread out, with Aklia opting to head in the westernmost direction. Her middle child, Amaya, hung close by, armed with two hand scythes that Angel Raphael created specifically for her grip. Noisy crickets and other critters roamed the bush, and Aklia sensed the recent presence of Cain's offspring. She stopped in the middle of the thicket, her heart pounding heavily in her chest.

"Is everything alright, Mother?" Amaya asked, swatting away at a gnat.

"Kneel to the ground and listen to the earth," Aklia instructed as she placed both hands onto the soft dirt and closed her eyes.

Amaya did as instructed and together, they witnessed the untold truth of Tati and Tyre.

The pair cackled with glee as Tati sank her teeth into the jugular of the frightened pregnant woman. Tyre tore into her arm as she struggled to resist the entities feeding from her. Tati released her, blood dripping from her mouth, down her chin, and onto her exposed bosom, looking every bit of the crazed and frightening creature that she was. She allowed her brother to continue feeding on the pregnant female while she snatched a young boy from behind the gate amidst a flock a sheep, he desperately attempted to hide behind. His screams echoed through the night. When she was done, she slung his small body back against the gate, causing the sheep to scatter. Tati and Tyre terrorized the small village, chasing the humans down into the bush, laughing hysterically in the night. One by one, the twins picked them off until by sunrise, nothing but maimed tortured flesh remained.

The earth revealed that the twins had indeed retreated to a small cave several miles north of where they stood. Amaya looked at her mother, terrified at the vision.

"By gods, Mother," Amaya gasped. "Go and retrieve your siblings and bring them here and be quick about it."

Amaya nodded. "Yes, Mother."

Aklia watched as her daughter took off, moving with the speed of a cheetah through the thicket. Unlike the rest of her children, Amaya had not been born with many gifts to make her an efficient Huntress. And after witnessing two of Cain's most wicked offspring, Aklia mentally noted to send Amaya back home to the blessed lands where she could protect the younger generations of Adam and Eve. Aklia could not bear to lose another one of her children to Cain and his abominations.

Tonight, the world would be a safer place when both Tati and Tyre's bones were buried deep in the ground.

***

The sun had begun its slow decline beneath the horizon as Cain approached another small village. Thankfully, his children had not reached this side of the country, but he knew that it would not be long before they did. He looked on as the small portion of humanity went about their daily lives, as a small girl trailed behind her mother who carried a ceramic bowl to the well just a few feet from where he stood. The woman's blood smelled rich, like the fertile soils of the Nile, and he knew that she would replenish the energy that he lost if he fed from her.

But, he didn't.

He simply watched, admiring the way she smiled and laughed at her daughter as the child skipped around her in singsong fashion, which made him think of his own wife, who waited for him at home. This was the image of life he yearned for, and perhaps for a time, he had it. Until his children expressed their need for blood, and all of the innocence that he craved to witness disappeared.

"You know, there are more of my kind coming," came a familiar voice from the ether.

Cain sighed. It had been quite a few centuries since the last time this entity spoke to him.

"I've watched you and those children of yours," the entity said. "And I must say that I am quite pleased. Things have turned out better than expected."

"And how so? You enjoy the fact that my children are terrorizing humanity and that we are damned and forever hunted?" Cain growled.

"No. As I told you before, your name will be of my legacy," the entity continued. "Your destiny is greater than anything this world has ever seen."

"I do not see how," Cain murmured. "Because of you, I have to hunt down my twins before my other daughter slaughters them herself. On top of that, my younger sister is tracking my entire family as we speak."

"Because of me, you are alive and a king among men. As a matter of fact, you are a god and have yet to step into your full glory."

"You know," Cain said evenly. "You never gave me your name."

"What's in a name?" the entity said as he manifested into a shadowy form. "You know who I am. You've always known."

"Still, what are you called other than—"

"Right now, I have no name. Man has no concept of who I am. Right now, I suppose I enjoy the name Set, and even Fallen One."

"I am not asking you for the name that man gave you," Cain growled. "I am asking you for the name that defines what you are."

"So that you can invoke me at will?" the entity replied with a smile.

"No."

"You have my blood. I think that is more than enough."

"Why are you here?" Cain asked, watching as the mother and daughter pair skipped off into the protection of the village.

"To warn you of what is to come," the entity said, his tone becoming more serious. "As I said, there are more of my kind coming for reasons I cannot explain. But when they do, the repercussions of their decisions will be nothing short of cosmic."

Cain raised an eyebrow. "How do you know?"

[79]

"Just because I no longer reside in the heavens does not mean I no longer have access to them."

"And why are you telling me this?"

"Because, if you are to continue my legacy, part of my job is ensuring your survival. When they come, you and your family will need to move to the far side of the earth and start anew. You will remain untouched if you do as I say."

The entity disappeared without another word and Cain continued to gaze out at the village, admiring the untouched serenity that this community offered.

"This place deserves to remain unmolested," he murmured under his breath. "As does the rest of mankind. Eliana knew this, and so do I."

Chapter Fifteen

"Mother, I must stand and fight with the rest of my siblings. It is my right and my honor," Amaya declared, gaining supportive nods from her brothers and sisters who gathered with her and Aklia.

"I cannot afford to lose you, my daughter. I will need you, Elan, and Moon to return to the blessed lands. Something tells me that you will be needed there," Aklia commanded.

"Those lands are protected by the Archangels themselves!" Elan protested, taking a stand. "I've wanted to put an end to Tyre's miserable life for years!"

"What we are about to do is disrupt the hornet's nest," Aklia began, her tone hardening. "Tati and Tyre are Cain's most lethal, although Eliana is not to be toyed with. But the twins are a sadistic pair and they will do things that Cain himself is disturbed by. If I die tonight, I need to rest in peace knowing that at least three of you can carry on the legacy. We have several more generations of Huntresses and protectors that need to be prepared for their missions in the world."

"But, Mother," Amaya cried. "I can—"

"The answer is no, Amaya," Aklia said firmly. "Now all three of you, go do as I say. We have no time."

Moon sighed and grabbed her sister's hand to do as instructed. Amaya cursed but turned around to leave, while Elan offered Aklia a hard stare.

"Should we survive the night, we will return and will continue to make strides in eradicating Cain's line, my son. This I promise you."

Elan said nothing and took off after his sisters.

Aklia glanced over at the remaining two children. Lana and Yam and said nothing.

However, it was Lana who spoke first.

"What is the strategy?"

"We go now, before they grow strong. Let's move!" Aklia took off running, her legs carried her across the plains like the wind. Her children followed behind her.

***

Tati lazily traced the bare skin of her twin's chest, admitting the definition of his pectorals. She gently placed a kiss on his nipple and slowly traced her fangs upward, towards his neck. He stirred but allowed her to continue.

"Where shall we go next?" she asked, sucking away at his neck.

"Wherever you want," he hissed as she sucked again. "The world is ours."

"The world is ours," she repeated.

Tyre's nostrils flared suddenly, and he sat up quickly, pushing Tati out of the way. His eyes flashed a deep crimson and his fangs crested. Tati picked up the scent and hissed. Both sprung to their feet and dematerialized out of the cave just in time to avoid being pierced in the chest by the tip of a long-handled spear. Tati materialized in front a family of trees and took a defensive position in front of Aklia.

Aklia swung her blade hard, barely missing Tati's head. Tati hissed and lunged forward, but Aklia was one step

[82]

ahead of her, and yanked Tati by her hair with enough force to snatch her backwards. Tati's body slammed into the large trunk of a nearby tree.

Meanwhile, Tyre snarled at Yam and Lana, who circled him. Tyre hissed violently and disappeared into the ether. Lana and Yam' senses focused on his energy and missed a sneak attack from behind them as he materialized. However, Tyre's split second distraction of glancing at his sister losing the battle to Aklia allowed Lana's battle ax enough time to separate his head from his shoulders.

Tati screamed as she witnessed her brother's body incinerate and out in the distance, both parties overheard the mournful wail of Cain. Lana and Yam rushed over to assist their mother. The brother and sister pair worked in tandem as Lana's foot connected with Tati's face, with Yam slamming a fist into her spine. The sound of Aklia's blade slicing through the air, cutting through Tati's skull, filled the clearing. It happened so quickly that Tati did not have time to scream.

The family of three stood frozen as Tati's remains became ash. Clouds quickly covered the sky and Aklia swallowed thickly as the first strike of lightning hit the trees several feet from where they stood. She looked at her children with full knowledge of the vengeance that was coming.

"Go," she urged them. "Quickly. And keep running. Cain is not a battle we will fight today. Keep running and do not look back."

The three of them launched off in the direction of the setting sun, moving with the speed of lightning. Aklia's prayers to the angels for protection covered them with an invisible shield, blocking Cain's senses. The roar that followed trailed them for miles until they reached the borders of the blessed lands.

Tonight, Aklia finally claimed success and she knew in time, there were many more victories to be won.

Chapter Sixteen

The heavens had no fury like the force of Cain as he tore through the bush after his sister and her children. She killed his twins! His Tati and Tyre! Yes, he would have dealt with them, but that was not *her* right to do so. After quietly disappearing from the village, he had already thought about the punishments for both Tati and Tyre. Both of them would have been dragged to separate corners of the earth, and in the deepest and tallest of mountains for a good century or two. But never, never could he fathom actually murdering his children, regardless of how monstrous they were. He believed he would beat Eliana to them, and he had hoped that in time, he could have convinced her to forgive, but instead, he found them dead.

His wretched sister, daughter of his awful stepfather Adam, had taken them away from him.

"You cannot run, Aklia!" he bellowed just as he was blinded by a shield of white light that stopped him in his tracks. "You cannot run! I will strip you of your spine, grind your teeth into powder and I will turn each of your children into the very thing you hate! All of your children, will be *mine*!"

He stopped running and sucked in deep breaths, trying to calm the rage that waged within him like a personal typhoon. He craved nothing but destruction. The pain in his heart cut deep and he could only imagine the pain that Luluwa would feel once she learned of what happened.

"One way or another, Aklia," he growled. "You will die by my hand, just as my children were killed by yours."

***

"You lie," Luluwa whispered, clutching his arm with such strength that her nails dug deep into his flesh. "Please tell me that you lie."

Cain gently pulled her hand away. "I wish, but I do not, my love. Tati and Tyre…they are gone."

Fresh tears filled her eyes as she gripped her swollen belly. "My children!"

Nunka growled while his wife looked on with sympathy. "So, it was Eliana that did this?"

Cain shook his head. "No. My sister did this. My sister, who has hunted us down for centuries has finally succeeded in taking not just one, but two of us out."

"Let me find her, Father," Nunka offered. "Please."

"Where she is, you cannot go, son," Cain stated, pulling a weeping Luluwa into his arms. "But I promise you son, I promise all of you that justice will be served."

"And what of Eliana?" Nunka asked. "She swore vengeance upon my siblings as well."

"Let her find peace," Cain said sadly. "We will deal with Eliana when the time comes. For now, we will remain on these lands until Luluwa gives birth and then it is best that we move on elsewhere."

"I hope you are not planning on leaving because of your sister!" Nunka snapped, his dark eyes glaring at his father.

"Aklia will be dead by my hand, so no," Cain said dryly. "And it would be wise for you to watch your tone, son. I

[86]

would hate for you to meet the intended fates of Tati and Tyre."

Nunka looked down while his wife turned her head. Luluwa wiped away her tears and grimaced. Beads of sweat formed at her brow as she clutched her stomach and doubled over.

"Luluwa!" Cain cried, kneeling down, taking her hand into his. "What's wrong?"

"The baby!" Luluwa screamed as she slid to the ground. "It's coming! It's coming!"

Nunka and Naima rushed to Luluwa's side to assist. Cain positioned himself in front of his wife, prepared to become her midwife, doctor, and coach. Luluwa rested her head on Naima's lap and cried out once more. She bit down hard on her lip, fighting back tears.

"Come on, Lu," Cain encouraged her. "Push. I can see the head."

Luluwa screamed again but did as she was told. In a long series of hard pushes, Luluwa's lungs nearly gave out from exhaustion as the sounds of a crying infant filled the air. Cain cradled the bloodied newborn to his chest, in awe of the enchanting green eyes that stared back at him.

"What did we have?" Luluwa whispered.

Cain smiled. "You gave me another daughter. On a full moon, a child with eyes the color of emeralds is born." He paused as he continued to gaze at the infant with awe. "We will call you Selene."

Luluwa smiled weakly while Naiama gently smoothed away her hair. "That's a beautiful name my love. Tati and Tyre would have loved her."

Cain rose to his feet, still cradling his minutes old daughter, and took her to the far side of the room, where he wrapped her in a blanket. Grief, anger, and joy fought for dominance in his system as he contemplated their next move. Aklia would surely pay for what she took from him. As a matter of fact, all of her descendants would pay for the sins committed this eve. He would see to it.

"Rest," Cain commanded his wife. "You have done well, and you have honored me, as always." He turned to face his son, Nunka, who still clung to his mother's side.

"Go feed, son. With your mother in this vulnerable condition, I do not trust that my sister will not attack again. We need to be strong."

Nunka sprung to his feet and nodded. "Yes, Father." He turned to his wife, Naima. "Watch over my mother."

"I will guard her with my life," Naima vowed.

Nunka disappeared as mist and took to the night, while Cain continued to stare into the eyes of his newborn daughter.

"I will protect you," Cain whispered to the infant. "This, I promise you."

Chapter Seventeen

Aklia, Yam, and Lana barely reached the border of the Blessed Lands just minutes before sundown. Amaya, Moon, and Elan overheard their arrival and rushed to greet them, lest Cain had found a way to cross the threshold.

"We were successful," Aklia huffed, bending down to catch her breath. "Tati and Tyre are no more."

"We took their heads!" Yam proclaimed. "Now our dear Seth can rest easy knowing that justice has been served."

"There will be no justice upon this earth until Cain and his abominations are gone," Aklia growled. "It is imperative that you all begin training those of our family that are of age and have manifested their gifts. They can no longer afford to sit idle on these protected lands when more blood will be shed."

"Seth's daughter, Nanari has the gift of fire and she is nearly as strong as Lana, Mother," Yam offered.

"Prepare her. Tomorrow prepare all of them." Aklia straightened her spine and began walking ahead, acknowledging the youngest members of her and Seth's tribe as she approached her two story dwelling built with mud and stone. "I must rest and commune with Spirit for guidance. Cain will not be denied retribution. He will come for each of us and then all of this will be for naught."

"But, Mother," Yam pressed. "We have him! He is weak! We should—"

"Do nothing. He is not weak. He is enraged. Do not be foolish. Celebrate this victory but prepare for war." Aklia walked away, her thoughts focused on all of the battles that led up to this point. The plan was to meet with Michael for assistance with a war strategy and intel on Cain's moves. The game had taken a more dangerous turn, and if she was going to win, she needed to prepare.

***

Cain watched an exhausted Luluwa rest her head against the bundle of sheep's skin as Selene took her breast. Both pride and sorrow filled him, as did rage. The slow burn of his rage simmered to the surface of his skin. Nunka had gone out in search of his sister Eliana, hoping to bring her back home to the family while Naima went out to hunt. He had no idea where he would relocate them. He just knew he would travel as far west as he could. And once Luluwa was safely tucked away, far from Aklia's reach, then there would be blood.

Aklia would not bring herself to hide in the Blessed Lands when there were still vulnerable human populations at risk for annihilation. No, she couldn't bear to sit back and watch as humanity suffered. He would draw her out, with her sword raised high above her head and into a certain death. And then, he would eradicate her children. Their names would be blotted out from history. What his dear sister took from him, he would take from her a thousand times over.

Selene's gentle breathing brought comfort to his enraged thoughts. He would forever mourn the loss of his twins. And with Eliana not here with them, he felt himself losing what was left of the humanity he clung to. Even while human, he was treated as a curse to his core family, the first humans, more so, by his own "father." Eve had done what she could to protect him, and even while he was banished from the Blessed Lands, she wanted to keep him safe. The only family that he had left were his precious Luluwa, Nunka, his wife Naima, Eliana, and now Selene.

Adam had inherited the earth and so had his sons. But he was no son of Adam.

And so, he, Cain, murderer of his brother, Abel, would take what was rightfully his as the rightful first- born son, and those who dared to stand in his way would pay dearly. No man, angel, nor Huntress would be able to stand against him.

Not even God himself.

Adam treated him as if he were a monster. The archangels hunted him as if he were the plague. And now his own blooded sister and her offspring wanted his head, and for what?

"Let them come," Cain growled, staring off into the dimming light. "Let them come."

Chapter Eighteen

The trek to the far side of the earth forced Cain and his family to move past mountainous regions that left little room even for a temporary lair. During this period, it was discovered that very few humans migrated this far north as the terrain proved to be barely habitable for most of the human populations. The icy winds sliced through them and for the first few nights of the journey, they were forced to feed on whatever animals they could find.

And still no Eliana.

Nunka had been unsuccessful in locating her. Her death had not registered in his senses. She had simply decided to not be found. Cain presumed that she could be anywhere on the planet and he wondered if she knew that Aklia and her minions had taken out the twins, Tati and Tyre.

The thought of their loss reminded him of the vengeance that he would unleash onto the planet. But instead of moving with the speed of an asteroid set on a collision course with earth, destroying any and everything in its path, he would infect the earth with darkness bit by bit, human by human, until every nook and cranny of this cursed planet quivered beneath his feet.

"How much farther are we to travel?" Nunka asked as he walked side by side with Cain. The females had fallen only slightly behind, with Luluwa being required to rest more. Selene's cries had lessened a few miles ago, and for that, Cain was thankful. Out of all of his children, Selene had been the most demanding. Aggression coursed through the infant's veins, and despite her now being a few days old, she grew now, resembling that of a six- month old human. Her green eyes were always aware, indicating a strong predatory nature. Cain could only imagine what she would be like when she reached full maturity.

"We still have quite a few moons, son," Cain said. "But I am certain that the mountains cannot go on forever."

"I could go on ahead of us," Nunka offered. "It would be faster to travel by air rather than foot."

"It would be. But we have both heavenly and earthly enemies. Your mother is still not at full strength and your sister is still young. You are needed here."

"Well, allow me to capture a couple of humans for us to consume," Nunka volunteered.

Cain considered his offer. With Luluwa needing to feed from his veins frequently to having to feed Selene from her own veins now, the blood of animals did not provide the strength his body needed. Human food was scarce in this region, which left him without options.

"Once we set up camp for the day, take Naima with you and bring back a couple of humans. Warriors preferably, being that their blood is strong."

Nunka nodded and the two marched on.

The tundra, a region of dry lands and hard ice during the winter months proved to be the greatest challenge. Nunka and Naima managed to capture at least two humans each night and bring them back alive for all of them to feed on. Here, there screams of terror could not be heard. And here it was where Cain learned of an innate ability to invade the human mind, bend its will, allowing them to feed in silence. Within days, the tundra became a graveyard of nightmarish reminders of their stay.

It was not long before they finally left those harsh lands and joined the untapped human ranks, hundreds of miles away from the Serpent River and the original grounds that both Cain and Adam walked. Glorious opportunity awaited. Here is where they would plan their strike. Here is where Luluwa and Selene would be kept safe.

And here is where Cain would create his army.

Lush greenery and the low-lying river that trickled south of where they stood welcomed them underneath the moonlight. Off in the distance, the powerful cries of large dogs echoed in the air. A small fire burned with the scent of roasting meat. A collective of human voices joined together in a mixed harmony of highs and lows in a joyful song. Cain listened, absorbing the beauty of this unknown side of humanity that branched off from Adam centuries ago. Here they had remained safe from Cain and his curse.

Until now.

"Tomorrow we will strike a bargain with the humans," Cain announced to his family.

"What?" Nunka hissed. "Why would we do that when we can take—"

"We are more than just night feeders, Nunka," Cain began. "We are the true gods of the earth and it is time that we act like it. We have remained hidden in the shadows of darkness for too long. And I want word to spread to my sister. I want her to taste the fear from the messages she receives of my rule. And once she does, her end and the end of her descendants will come."

"What will we do until then?"

Cain turned to look at his hot -headed son. Dark eyes stared back at him with curiosity. "Our destinies begin tomorrow, son. Just watch."

***

Aklia watched her nieces and nephews spar with growing concern. Yam clutched the spear, and with lightning speed, knocked his twelve -year old nephew on his back. The boy released a hard groan before he hit the ground. Yam hovered over him before offering his hand. Aklia released a hard sigh.

"Get up, Amir," she barked, snatching the spear from Yam's hand. "Again."

Amir glanced at his uncle with uncertainty. His dark eyes filled with unshed tears as he reluctantly accepted his uncle's hand and stood on shaky knees to brace himself. His great aunt, Aklia shook her head with frustration. The last thing she wanted was for any of her children, grandchildren, nieces, and nephews to have to continue the fight against Cain and his blood drinkers. She believed that the Curse would end by her sword-- the same sword that Archangel Michael had given to her so that her children would not have to bear the burden of this legacy. Adam believed in her too, and before his soul transitioned to the next world, he looked at her with pride and hope in his eyes, with faith that she would slay the demon son that plagued his family.

Meanwhile, her mother Eve, despite remaining silent, sent out a plea through her eyes for Aklia to show mercy on her brother and sister. At one point, Aklia might have been inclined to do so. But Cain had already taken away so much from all of them, that mercy was a thing that no longer existed. Cain's existence needed to be wiped away from the earth's memory.

"Again, Amir," she commanded after a long pause.

This time, when Yam lunged forward, Amir dodged the sudden move with precision, flipping out of the way just as Aklia had taught him. Aklia watched as the two went back and forth with the sparring for a few minutes before walking away to be alone with her thoughts.

She could sense Cain somewhere off in the far distance, destroying whatever part of the world he trekked to. But she knew it would not be long before he would resurface and when that time came, she would be ready.

Chapter Twenty

Cain did exactly as he had promised the Elder. By nightfall, he and his son Nunka and Nunka's wife, Naima melted into the shadows of the Eastern tribes and spared no one. Screams of terror ripped through the otherwise silent night. Many of the men fought bravely, but bones were still snapped like twigs; necks were ripped through, entrails were spilled, and by dawn, Cain dragged the last of the Eastern tribe's dying chief to the feet of the tribal Elder and his sons.

"Tell me what you wish for me to do with him," Cain growled, his eyes illuminating a deep crimson. Blood covered his face and his chest, making him appear more horrifying than normal.

The tribal Elder swallowed thickly, his hands trembling as they covered his mouth. "I- I- I…"

"Remember, this is the leader who permitted his men to steal from you, to rob you and your people of peace. His men violated your women, killed your men…and for the women, how can you be sure that through the rape, life sustained itself and the blood of thine enemies is raised on your lands, without your knowledge?"

The struggling chief attempted to pull away, but Cain quickly shoved his head into the dirt and pressed down on him with his foot.

"I could easily break his skull or…" Cain began slowly. "We could set him free to tell the story to the neighboring clans of all that he witnessed. His wounds would be part of the testimony of all that transpired this eve."

The tribal Elder looked down at the badly beaten man. Lacerations covered his face and neck, his arm barely remained attached to his shoulder, and with each shallow breath, there was an indication of broken ribs. The tribal Elder was filled with regret.

As if he truly had a choice in the matter.

"Let him go," the tribal Elder said hoarsely.

Cain scoffed, but slowly lessened the weight of his foot on the man's head. "Mercy is for the weak and soon I will teach your sons what it means to truly rule."

The man screamed as Cain snatched him up on his feet to stand. "You will go the north and speak of all that took place against your people. Tell them my name and warn them of my pending arrival."

The tribal Elder and his sons looked on in silent terror as the wounded warrior began to stumble forward, anxious to put as much distance between himself and Cain as possible, even if it had to be one step at a time.

"And my name is Cain," he called out.

But the warrior did not turn around. He just continued to limp forward in the direction he was ordered to go, unbeknownst to him, Nunka would ensure that he did as he was instructed.

They watched him until he disappeared into the thicket. Silence as dense as the cumulous clouds that took form in the sky hovered over the group. The tribal Elder and his sons learned first of the evil their people had aligned themselves with. As if sensing their fear, Cain glanced over at the tribal Elder, studying his fair features. He had brown skin with red undertones when he stood underneath the harsh light of the sun, and straight, snow white hair that covered his back like silk. His robing was made from goat skin that covered his withering frame perfectly. His sons shared the same complexion and lean build, slanted chestnut eyes, and the intricate marking of their tribe that littered their bare chests.

"Now, that I have fulfilled my end of the bargain," Cain said, breaking the silence. "We need to address how your people will fulfill yours."

Aklia

Five years later…

"It has been too quiet for too long," Yam said to his mother. "We have all but eradicated Eliana's creations, which is good. But there is still no sign of her or Cain."

"We will find her eventually." Aklia sighed. "Or she will find us. And as for Cain, I already know what he has been up to. He will be coming soon. I feel it. Prepare to lead those who will not be joining us in battle to the hills for safety. Raphael has already blessed those grounds where Cain and his monsters are unable to cross. That will be your fallback position."

Yam frowned. "Yours too, right?" He knew his mother and for the last few nights, she seemed to have mentally withdrawn into herself. Cain had haunted her since birth, despite being a plague on his bloodline. But instead of Adam taking the helms in avenging his family, Aklia had been the one to do it. Seth, on the other hand, chose the quiet life, as did the other children of Adam and Eve. None of them possessed the courage or the will to fight, which is why the angels armed Aklia with special abilities that her children inherited to assist with the fight against Cain and his cursed family.

But something was different. On the surface, Aklia stood composed and at the ready like a seasoned warrior, but her eyes held a silent resignation. The fiery determination she once held no longer existed, and that was what worried him.

"Just remember everything that I taught you and your siblings and make sure Lana and the baby are safe. She is to be the next generation. Even if I defeat Cain, his legacy has already begun, and his children will still continue. Humanity will always be at risk."

"Yes, Mother." Yam nodded. "But you still didn't answer my question."

Aklia sighed. "Son, I am too tired to answer any of your questions. I need to rest."

Yam turned to leave, but just as his back faced his mother, she said, "I love you, my son. I love all of my children, including Adinkra still, though she is now in spirit. Now go."

Yam nodded and stepped foot out of the large mud dwelling that his family built to give his mother some space to rest. Aklia stretched out on the layered blankets made of sheepskin and wool. Her muscles ached from years of battle and though she'd reached the age of three hundred, with all of the youth and physicality of a young woman, she knew that she was not immortal. She had been allowed to live as long as she had for the mere purpose of defeating Cain. But Gabriel had already informed her in a dream that she would not survive the battle. Unfortunately, Cain's legacy had become part of a much larger and grander plan, and she was simply the catalyst for the next destined Huntress.

She wondered if that Huntress would be one of her own daughters, Lana, Amaya, or Moon. Next to Adinkra, Amaya had grown to become a fierce fighter in her own right. Amaya possessed the gift of elemental workings, meaning she could manipulate the weather, create fire with the simple flick of her wrist, and even speak to the earth. Lana's gift rested with communicating with the animals,

[101]

while Moon possessed strong psychic abilities that intensified when the moon was full, hence the name.

If not one of her own tribe, would this Huntress be someone of the distant future? A future that neither she nor her children would be a part of? How much darker would the world have to become before humanity could be saved? How many lives would have to be lost, ruined even, before the Light said enough? These questions and many more weighed heavily on Aklia as she closed her eyes and struggled to drift off into a desperately needed sleep.

Chapter Twenty- One

It seemed as if it took no time for the small tribe to blossom into a growing empire. In less than three years, Cain with the support of Nunka, Naima, and Luluwa, the northern most region of Mesopotamia had been conquered. The land had become known as the Red Desert from the blood spill, and night after night, Nunka and Naima bathed in the blood of the innocent.

No dwelling was safe, nor gender, and no weapon formed against them would succeed. Temples were being built to honor the "god" Cain, with the hope that in the sacrifice of a few, the many could be spared. The tribe that Cain protected and claimed as his own had quadrupled in size and would soon become the first city of Cain's kingdom.

Finally, he could live the life he deserved after so many years of wandering like a nomad with no real home to call their own. His army was slowly forming, the army that he would use to stand against Aklia. She would pay for all of the grief she caused his family, for Tati and Tyre's lives, she would pay with her own. Her children and grandchildren would watch the matriarch of their family tree crumble and fall before them. His blood drinkers, his Night Men humans he deemed as worthy of his bite and transformation- would all march into battle at his command against his sister and everything that she loved.

So far, there were only ten. The first hundred or so were unsuccessful, some of them simply being physically unable to survive the transformation, unlike his wife Luluwa. Those who did survive however, had to be exterminated due to "blood rage." It was in these morbidly dark moments when Cain understood the true affect his bite held on his victims.

Through Luluwa, he learned those bitten were unable to withstand the sun, could not sustain physical food, and required increased amounts of blood in comparison to his intake. Luluwa could shape shift just as well as he could in whatever animal she chose, which was often an owl, but she preferred to remain in her human form. Over time, he watched her become the dark Huntress that he adored. During their hunts, she could throw her voice to confuse humans and she possessed the strength of at least ten men.

He supposed that her feeding mostly from his veins had tempered the blood rage. At this rate, the human populations would be wiped out within a matter of days. Hence, the ten that survived were those who fought against that primal urge to kill and responded to his command. And it was also in these moments that Cain began to understand his link – the invisible chord that tied them to him. He sensed them even when he was not consciously aware. It was like his family tree had now been split in half: by birth and by bite.

Nunka had not been permitted to recruit for his own army of Night Men. The only extension of Cain's son was his wife, Naima, and controlling her had always been of difficulty. Cain examined the tallest of his Night Men as they stood out on the high steps of the nearly completely built temple. The moonless sky was littered with the silent flickering of stars that hung above them. The deep valley seemed to have adopted the same silent attitude of the stars, as there was not a single sound that could be heard, and for Cain, it was not yet to be considered late. The locals had retreated into their dwellings in fear. Not one animal bayed, growled, or peeped, for it seemed that they too disappeared in fear.

"Geb," Cain said to his tallest warrior. The giant stood at nearly nine feet, easily towering over Cain's six-foot six frame.

"Yes, my lord?" Geb uttered reverently. "I am here to do as you wish."

"Excellent," Cain replied, pleased. "Have you fed?"

Geb swallowed. "No."

"When was the last time you've taken blood?"

"Many nights," Geb replied.

"Do you hunger?"

Geb nodded. "Yes."

"What if I told you to starve another night?" Cain asked, his expression unreadable.

"Then I will," Geb pledged.

Cain paused. Geb represented a hope and a light for a future he had only dreamed of: his children of the night born through bite, dominating humanity, with him standing at the helm of it all as god.

"Take your men with you," Cain commanded. "Feed and feed well. Soon you will have more brothers to train."

Geb said nothing as he bowed his head in gratitude.

"Go," Cain barked.

Geb shot to feet and took off running at full speed out of the temple. Nunka had taught him well and Cain would be sure to reward his son handsomely when all was said and done. But before he could accomplish his grander ambitions, he needed to permanently remove the thorn in his side.

Aklia.

He knew that she still hunted. Her children and grandchildren had entered the world with the same mission and purpose, to eradicate his kind. Night after night he felt the deaths of his children, their lives turned to ash by the tips of Aklia's blade.

Upon Geb's return, the attack on Aklia would commence. She would bleed out by nightfall, as would her children and her children's children.

Cain smiled as he glanced around the interior of his temple. An abstract image of him with his mouth opened wide, exposing both his top and bottom sets of fangs dripping with blood captured his attention on the incomplete mural. In time, he hoped that the humans he spared would see him as their savior and protector and sing him songs of worship that continued forever.

But as long as Aklia lived another day to fight his name could only be whispered in the darkness of night.

And that had to change.

Chapter Twenty - Two

Aklia opened her eyes, annoyed at the brightness of the sunlight. Her body hummed with sudden awareness, her intuition alarming her to the finality of all that she had trained for had arrived. She knew it like she knew her name that the next chapter in the book of life had begun. She trained her children and grandchildren their entire lives for this. They knew what to do. She loved them, cared for them, fought for them, and those that survived, would continue on with her legacy. The Archangels would protect them, and it was Archangel Michael himself that ensured her that her bloodline would survive well beyond the future centuries, which was all the reassurance she needed to make peace with herself.

Rolling onto her side, she smiled at Bandi, the youngest of Lana's children, who loved to crawl into bed with her and sleep. Bandi loved to rest next to her grandmother and told her so on a constant now that she could speak fluently and with understanding. Aklia gently kissed the child on top of the head, inhaling her warm, natural scent. Bandi smelled of earth: the flowers, the grass, whatever her small body could roll in after her mother finished her bath. And as much as Lana scolded her for such behavior, Aklia could not love her anymore. The child was so full of life and brilliance, that Aklia could never be too angry with her.

She quietly pushed herself up from the bedding, careful not to wake the child. For three centuries, Aklia wondered if this war between herself and her brother would continue into eternity. But as her vision became clearer, before she raised her sword for the last time, she would be sure to pass the information as it related to her fate on to her children.

After tonight, it would be their responsibility to continue to pave the way until the birth of the destined Huntress.

Again, she took another look at Bandi, the child's creamy brown complexion reminded Aklia of the riverbanks of the Nile, so rich with life as the earth itself. Bandi possessed such a playful and magnetic spirit, one could not help but find themselves excited to be in her presence. But Bandi would only live her life as a normal human. From what Aklia could tell, the child possessed no extrasensory gifts like her mother and siblings. As a matter of fact, a few of Aklia's grandchildren were born without gifts, something that both troubled and delighted her. Either way. all of whom shared her bloodline would either fall victim or become victorious in a world where blood drinkers existed. How would a human such as Bandi protect herself?

And then it dawned on her. Soon the day would come to an abrupt end, and in a few hours her children would begin to execute the plan that she strategized many months ago. She had served the Light since she could walk, absorbed all of the knowledge and teachings of the Archangels, and fought bravely in the shadows of humanity. Yet, through it all, she asked for nothing. But as worry for Bandi and the other children like her grew, Aklia fell to her knees, a single tear slid down her cheek as she whispered, "Archangel Michael, please I need a word with you."

A few minutes dragged on before she sensed the gentle presence of an entity behind her. The soft glow of his light warmed her like the warmth of the fire on winter nights. Peace flooded her veins, vanquishing all thought of worry.

"Whatever it is you need, Aklia," Archangel Michael began. "I am here."

"I need your help," Aklia whispered.

"Tell me."

***

Aklia stood at the ready near the base on the outskirts of their encampment. Her children: Amaya, Elan, Moon, and Yam stood with her. Her pregnant daughter, Lana had been sequestered away with the rest of the family, which stretched out to well over two hundred. The older grandchildren who were trained to fight amounted to around fifteen, each of them positioned in various points of the nearly vacant site that had been their family home for centuries.

The lands of Adam had protected them since the Curse of Cain; however, these same lands had kept them isolated. Everything seemed to be going according to plan. Archangel Raziel divided the family up into several groups and directed them towards various parts of the world. Some were to head towards the mountains, while others were sent to the jungles of the southern regions. Some were sent to the deserts while others were guided towards the high tides of the seven seas.

Aklia silently mourned the division of her family tree. They were being separated by the root. a strategy that she understood all too well. There was a much bigger plan at stake, and as she watched the sun made its slow retreat beneath the horizon, she wondered what exactly that plan could be. How did they all fit into this cosmic grand scheme of things? How would it all play out? The shift in the atmosphere happened almost instantly. Her senses heightened, and with the visual acuity of an eagle, she spotted subtle movement in the trees. One by one she felt

[109]

them, Cain's children and the members of his army, materializing into solid form, but with the sun clinging to its last few moments of light, she knew instantly that these entities had to wait until complete darkness.

But there was no sign of Cain.

"I can feel them, Mother," Yam whispered. "And they have fed."

"We wait, son," Aklia told him. "Do not rush into anything. For all we know, this could be a set up for an ambush."

Quickly, Aklia sent out a mental message to her small army: *Do not move. Wait until I give the signal. This might be a set up.*

She returned her gaze to the trees and waited as the sun continued to set. From what she could gather, there were at least ten blood drinkers, high off the blood of their victims. She did not dare underestimate the fact that there could be more. Eliana's careless feedings had created a nearly unstoppable surge of blood drinkers that wiped out several small clans just east of where they were. It had taken a few years for Aklia and her children to eradicate them and send Eliana off in another direction. Therefore, Aklia could only imagine the carnage that Cain and his brood had left behind. Rumor of the Blood Kingdom, as it was called, reached her ears, setting fire to her blood. She vowed that before she died, she would at least take out her sister Luluwa or Nunka's wretched wife, Naima.

One of those females had to go.

She swallowed thickly, her grip on her blade tightening as the sky continued to darken. Night creatures had grown silent, as if they knew what was about to take place and wanted no part of the pending bloodshed. As the sky succumbed to total darkness, her vision had never been more acute as it was now. She felt the ground tremble as the leaves in the trees began to rustle. Yam reached for his arrows that he carried on his back and readied his bow. Aklia's jaw clenched the instant the entity materialized in front of her, fangs exposed, blood dripping from his chin.

Cain prepared them for what he perceived as his sister's weaknesses. He never considered her strength. Her son's arrow reached its target, the silver tip piercing the entity's heart as her hard swing took off the creature's head. Ash hit the wind and the stench of sulfur claimed her nostrils.

"Attack!" she roared into the darkness.

As if on cue, another blood drinker whizzed past her, appearing as nothing but a blur towards her daughter, Moon. Moon's palms crackled with an electric blue energy that she used to bind the entity with like a rope. The blood drinker collapsed to the ground, struggling to fight against the electric cord that burned through its flesh. With lightning speed, Moon's silver blade sliced through its neck, severing the head.

More ash filled the air.

Silver tipped arrows clouded the sky and rained down on the blood drinkers that rushed forward. Screams ripped through the air, but none of it deterred Aklia from moving forward. The scream that sliced through the darkness chilling scream from her granddaughter, Takiya, forced her to turn back however, as a thickly built blood drinker bit into her neck.

Elan and his nephew Set rushed to her aid, both filling the blood drinker's back with arrows while Aklia's short blade went straight into its neck. The creature released Takiya instantly before turning to ash. Set carried Takiya off to the safety of the hills. Aklia knew she would recover – none of her children would meet the Curse of Cain – but nonetheless it still hurt her heart to witness them hurt.

Rage fueled her as she back flipped out of the reach of a giant, whose fangs were of saber tooth proportions. Off in the distance, she sensed the dark energy of Cain moving forward. But another entity quickly captured her attention.

Naima.

Lightning struck as the female took form just a few yards away from Aklia. The two combatants locked eyes and lunged on a sure-fire collision course. Yam, Moon, Amaya, and Elan continued to slaughter the few remaining blood drinkers that were now attempting to retreat. Naima disappeared into the ether at the last second, barely missing Aklia's blade. Aklia double backed, unmoved by the sudden move. She froze, using her heightened senses to pinpoint Naima's exact location, but was caught by a surprise punch to the back, which knocked her forward. Aklia caught herself before she hit the ground, using the tip of her blade to regain balance. Naima hissed, her talons taking a hard swipe at Aklia, who in turn shoved the sole of her foot into the blood drinker's chin.

Aklia felt Nunka materialize close by as well as another blood drinker. The hard whir of a battle ax whizzed past her shoulder, barely grazing it, and slammed into the center of the unaware male's chest, instantly turning him to ash. Nunka hissed and took cover while Naima continued to engage Aklia in battle. Aklia overheard the telepathic message sent from Yam to Amaya, as both rushed toward Nunka, who idly watched from the clearing.

Deep crimson eyes glared at them from the darkness and the two siblings worked in sync against Cain's oldest son. Amaya opened her palms, creating a band of white light, which she shot directly at the entity. Nunka hissed again and folded away into the darkness. Aklia watched it all unfold in slow motion as she dodged another swipe from Naima. Her son spun around quickly to find himself trapped in the death grip of Nunka's large hands. Amaya ran at full speed towards her brother, but even with all of the speed of the cosmos, she was not fast enough to stop what happened next.

Nunka tightened his grip on the younger male's neck and snapped it. The hard crunch of her son's trachea being broken ripped through her. And to further add insult to injury, Nunka dug his talons into the dead man's back and snatched out his spine. White hot rage and blackened grief tore at her, transforming her into a darker version of the Huntress that gave the blood drinkers pause.

"My son!" Aklia cried out. "My son!"

Amaya, still running at full speed, slammed her body into Nunka, knocking the wind and her brother's remains out of his grip. In a fit of fury, she took her blade constructed purely of bronze and gifted to her from her grandfather Adam and sliced off Nunka's leg. The blood drinker did not turn to ash, but black blood spurted from the wound as he hit the ground.

I got him, Mother! Amaya thought to her mother. *Take out his wife*!

[113]

Lightening crackled in her palms as she gripped her blade. The handle cut through her hands and her own blood dripped down the handle, which disoriented her.

"Naima!" Nunka called out with failing strength. "Get back!"

Naima, crazed by the scent of Aklia's blood, took another lunge towards the enraged Huntress.

"Naima!"

Nunka's cries were too late. With all of her strength, Aklia's blade connected with the crown of Naima's head in a downward motion. Naima stared blankly at Aklia before her body broke apart in two halves, turning to ash as it hit the ground. Nunka looked on in disbelief, and as Amaya prepared to land the death blow, he was snatched away into the ether by his mother, Luluwa.

A black tornado touched down out of nowhere, thickening the blanketing darkness.

"Take cover!" Elan shouted in the distance.

"Use the elements to shield yourselves!" Aklia hollered back. "Amaya! Go!"

Amaya ran over to her mother, her face bruised and the rest of her bloodied and battered. "I won't leave you."

Aklia grabbed her daughter's arm and shoved her in the direction of her brother. "Go now! You will all be needed later to fight. But for now, this is my fight."

"I don't want to lose you!" Amaya cried. "Please! Let me stand and fight with you!"

"I refuse to lose another child to that bastard!" Aklia growled. She looked at her daughter, her heart swelling with love. So many years spent training her, preparing her for a legacy that she would have never chosen for any of her children. So much pain and grief stared back at her.

Memories of Amaya crawling around as an infant, laughing at her father, Ram who teased her with funny faces every night while Aklia would take leave to hunt. Images of her children gathered around her, listening to her stories of The Almighty and what it meant to serve the Light. Amaya, out of all her children, held the most courage and also the deepest loyalty to her mother.

Aklia quickly snatched her daughter into a tight embrace, and a silent knowing passed between them. Tears filled Amaya's eyes as she held on to her mother.

"Be strong my beautiful, Amaya. Carry my blade when all is done and carry it well. I will always be with you," she whispered.

"I don't understand." Amaya sniffled. "This is not just!"

"You will understand in time. Do not be of angry with the angels, nor Him Above. Tell your siblings the same. But this, this has to be done."

"Please, Mother. You do not have to do this!"

"I must. One way or another, what was written long before must come to pass. I love you, Amaya. Now go. Cain will forever remember this battle. I need you to be strong for your siblings. *Go!*"

Aklia shoved Amaya towards her brother and watched as she stumbled, heartbroken and overrun with grief, towards him. Orbs of light followed her, giving Aklia comfort in knowing that those of her bloodline would always be protected by the archangels – including Bandi.

"Cain! Son of the Fallen! Betrayer of the Most High," Aklia seethed through clenched teeth. "Slayer of your own blood! I challenge you."

"You have taken what is mine," Cain's voice boomed from the tornado. "And for that, you will pay."

"As you have taken what is mine," Aklia growled, gripping the handle of her sword.

"When I am done with your carcass, I will turn the bones of all of your children into dust," Cain said as the tornado's speed slowly decreased, and the winds began to dissipate.

"Do it," Aklia challenged swinging her blade with expert precision.

Cain's laughter echoed across the field as he materialized into physical form. "Come on, little sister. I'm tired of these games. Let's finish this."

Chapter Twenty -Three

Cain

His sister met him the instant he took form. Her blade met his in a steel against steel match that seemed to extend forever. Any other human would have been easily defeated, but Aklia reminded him with each hard strike that she was not an ordinary human. Her strength matched his, as did her rage. Blow for blow, they fought. Barreling through the open field, knocking down trees that stood as silent sentinels. From the earth, he called forth the forces of darkness to ensnare her, but she countered with the forces of Life for protection.

He would have loved her had she not become what she was.

She possessed his mother Eve's gentle face and beautiful almond shaped eyes. Her lean build came from Adam, as did her temper, but still he had always found her to be magnificent. Had she come to him with diplomacy rather than her sword, he would have protected her from his kind. He would have made sure that all her children and children's children and their children would have never known of the Darkness that he lorded over. He would have always kept them in the light.

But Adam and his forces of protectors of Light ruined her and destroyed their bond before one could have been properly formed. She hated him since birth, even though it would be many, many years before he truly wronged her. Because of her, he lost two of his own children and maybe a third, as Nunka rested on his deathbed. Because of her Nunka lost a mate. Because of her, the humans sang her songs of praise while they cowered at the mere mention of his name.

All of this would soon end with her.

She ran up the side of the tree and backflipped out of his way, barely missing his blade. How was this even possible? What kind of Divine Intervention allowed her to escape his wrath? How was it that she held special gifts that only her children would inherit? He swung again with his fist, punching a tree instead of her face. He dematerialized into the ether, while telekinetically uprooting a giant tree root and tripping her with it. She stumbled forward, but quickly sprang to her feet.

"Admit defeat, Aklia," Cain's voice rumbled through the trees. "And I might be kind enough to allow you to live."

"Never!" Aklia declared, landing a hard punch to his face as he materialized in front her. The force of her blow knocked him backwards into a small stream. "You are a living curse! A blight upon the name of Adam."

The mere mention of Adam's name sent him over the edge with fury. He retaliated by yanking her by her foot and upper cutting her to the jaw. Her head snapped back, her eyes rolled to the back of her head, leaving her temporarily dazed.

"You will never again speak his name!" he bellowed.

Aklia, was up on her feet by sheer will and blocked another blow from him. Her hands crackled with energy and she landed a strike to his neck, hitting him with the force of lightening. She became motion , and as she prepared to land the kill blow with her sword when Luluwa materialized from out of nowhere, and the two of them engaged.

"Little sister," Luluwa cooed, dodging a swing.

"I will take your head too!" Aklia swore.

"Luluwa get back!" Cain commanded his wife as Aklia advanced on her. "No!"

Cain forced himself up off the wet ground and rushed over to join the battle. Luluwa had never been a fighter. He had always protected her, keeping her as far away from harm as possible. Witnessing her attempt to engage with a warrior as seasoned as Aklia terrified him to no end.

Luluwa, probably sensing the pending danger, tried to dematerialize. However, without a blink, Aklia flung a small, silver dagger at her target. Luluwa mistakenly turned around to face her. In the split second before the dagger pierced her chest, her gaze met Cain's and instant grief claimed him. The dagger disappeared into her bosom, striking her heart, and in horror, Cain witnessed his wife crumble to dust.

"*No!* Luluwa! My Luluwa!" Cain bellowed.

A gentle breeze swept up her remains and carried her off into the darkness.

Aklia clutched her blade and prepared for the onslaught. Cain's rage fell to abysmal depths, his eyes blackened, his fangs elongated, and his body bulked, giving him the appearance of an enraged bull.

"You. Will. Pay." Cain's growl deepened and the pitch darkness that surrounded them thickened.

[119]

Aklia narrowed her gaze. "As will you."

Cain's roar rattled the trees and with speed too quick for the human eye. He and Aklia collided into one another. The swift chime of her blade against his broke the silence of night, shattering his blade into hundreds of pieces. The power punch that he landed sent her flying backwards, knocking the wind out of her.

He would tear her apart, limb from limb. He would mount her head on a pike for all of her children to bear witness to. For Tati and Tyre. For Naima. For his son. For Luluwa.

He roared again at the thought of his wife. She came when he needed her, this time to protect him, and he failed her. Selene would grow up without her mother.

He approached Aklia slowly. He would enjoy this, relish every moment of snatching out her entrails. He would savor the moment of victory as he pressed his foot to her skull and felt it explode under the weight of his foot. And her children, the Most High, would be the only source of protection – the archangels be with them. Tears flooded his eyes as Aklia struggled to find her balance.

"It didn't have to be this way," Cain growled as he inched closer.

The first rays of the sun began to creep over the horizon, forcing its way through the treetops. Adam had always treated him like a monster, so he would become exactly that.

Aklia lunged again, only for him to smack her down to the ground. Each time she attempted to rise, he leveled a fist to her head, and still, she would not break.

"I refuse for my children to befall a legacy such as this," she murmured through a bloodied and swollen lip. Her nose was broken, both of her once beautiful eyes blackened and swollen. Her blood dripped to the earth and still she stood against him, how poetic.

"I did not ask for this," he told her.

"Neither did I," she said as she found the strength to stand. She swung again and missed as he ducked out of the way. She doubled back with a series of successful punches, while he returned a few of his own. Exhaustion began to claim her. Tired of the games, Cain's fist connected with her temple just as she flung her sword. The instant her sword left her hand, he watched as her life essence separated from her body. Her lifeless, glossy eyes stared back at him as she collided into a giant tree, while her sword remained steadfast.

Cain felt the metal impale his heart, all the way through to his spine. The metal scorched his flesh like acid and in the few moments he had to cling to life, he thought of Luluwa, the fabric of his soul, his peace, and his sanity. He remembered her kindness towards him when Adam was at his cruelest. He remembered how she dared to run away with him the night following his brother's murder. Her beautiful spirit still remained intact even upon her transition into a blood drinker. She refused to feed on women or children, only demonstrating her violent streak when necessary. Her beauty would forever be ingrained in his memory.

And poor Selene. Who would protect her from the humans whom he ruled over? Once his death was discovered, Selene would be killed to prevent her from reaching maturity. And Eliana, wherever she was, he hoped that she would continue to thrive. His legacy would be her own. Out of all of his children, Eliana stood out and he admired her for her strength and tenacity.

As he fell to his knees, blood dripped onto his hands, spilling from his wound. He took another look around him, reminding himself how lonely the embrace of death was. Aklia fought him with everything she had without fear, and even as she stood face to face with death, never cowered or begged for mercy. No, she accepted her fate while exacting her vengeance. It would be many years before Cain would reflect on this moment. Aklia defined what it would mean to be a Huntress, and it would be almost a millennia before he encountered another of her ilk and strength.

How was it fair that one never asks to be born, much less be born to the circumstances that would forever define his path, and still find himself punished for decisions made? How? How was it fair that he suffered punishments for the sins of his mother and the resentment of his father for a crime committed long before he was even a thought? How was it that he, the first born of woman and not from the earth, be subjected to a curse that none knew existed? Never was he good enough for the Creator, nor for the person he long believed to be his father. The only person who readily accepted him as he was had been reduced to ash. Perhaps there was life beyond the physical. Maybe he would be permitted freedom from this world as he too was weary of it all: the running, the shame, the hiding, the thirst for blood…

Maybe, Aklia had actually set him free.

Or maybe, it was only the beginning.

Part III

Genesis

Chapter Twenty- Four

Several weeks later

"I started to believe that you would never wake up again," came a familiar melodic voice that hovered over him

Slowly awareness began to creep in, and the cool, dank air that surrounded him chilled his skin. Sudden flashes of his last few moments with Luluwa just before Aklia's dagger pierced her heart forced his eyes opened. He sucked in a deep breath with a snarl as he shot up, frantically surveying his surroundings. The pain in his chest where Aklia's sword had struck him registered with a sharp reminder that he had yet to fully heal, forcing him to lay back down.

"Where am I?" Cain demanded.

"Underground, for now," the entity told him. "It's safer."

"What are you talking about?" Cain demanded. "I need to return to what is left of my family."

"Sorry. Can't allow you to return to the surface at this time," the entity said coolly. "And as far as your family goes, Eliana and Selene are here. Nunka is too, but quite frankly, he would have been better off being left where he was."

"Where are they? Tell them to come to me. We have much to discuss."

"I will soon. But there are things you need to know and prepare for when you return to the surface."

"Why are we underground?" Cain asked, staring at the stalagmite that hung above his head. Above he could hear the loud crash of ocean waves pounding against each other. Beneath him, he could sense the presence of the disembodied spirits wandering about, some of them crying out for help, while others simply drifted.

"Where are we exactly?"

"Let's just say I am still in the pupa stages of empire building. You should be thanking me."

"And why would I thank you?" Cain frowned.

The entity's dark form emerged from the shadows just enough to offer Cain more visibility. Dark hair that hung loosely passed his shoulders, a pair of unreadable colorless eyes stared back at him, bronze skin stretched out over a frame that stood over six feet, while clinging to over two hundred pounds of raw muscle. And from Cain's line of vision, he made note of the similar shape of nose, mouth, and chin…It was no wonder Adam hated him.

"I saved you. Aklia's blade struck you down sure and true, and had you not carried my blood, your reign would have surely come to an end," the entity informed him. "You have been in a regenerative sleep for weeks now, and during that period, much has transpired."

"Such as?"

The entity smiled. "For starters, a mutiny was sparked in the heavens, unbeknownst to you many years ago. While you were galivanting about in the world, seeking to build your own empire, those of my kind came down to join the humans, most of them curious about their baser natures. Humans demanded answers to questions to things unseen and in turn, my brothers mingled and made themselves gods amongst men. They taught them things, things that I never considered to teach, and as a result, the Veil that

[125]

separates the heavens from the humans has been prematurely breached. Hybrids, half human, half angel, were born and created another imbalance, which is why I believe that you are the greatest creation."

"So, there are others like me?" Cain asked curiously.

"No. Not quite. Some were much more horrific, but all of them were solely focused on feeding their lusts. Which brings us to why we are hundreds of feet beneath the earth's surface. The Heavens sent a flood, washing away all forms of life with the exception of a few, and right now they are heavily protected. Even I cannot visit upon them."

"And what of Aklia's descendants. Her bloodline?"

"That I do not know. But there is no place on earth that is not flooded with the wrath of the sea. When I found you, the rains began. The humans had been caring for Selene in your absence, while Eliana searched for you and her mother. When I realized what was happening, I brought all of you down here for safety."

Cain closed his eyes and released another hard sigh. Memories of Luluwa's beautiful face, so much like that of his mother, brought tears to his eyes. Luluwa was gone. Tati was gone. Tyre was gone. His mother, the only other person besides Luluwa to love him unconditionally was gone. Adam hated him since birth, while Abel, his brother had been the thorn in his side that he thought he would never be able to get rid of. Abel was the sun, the center of his family's universe, and Cain had stripped them of their light. Aklia was the blade, the sword of Adam, his executioner, avenger and protector.

And he killed both of them.

[126]

"I suppose I owe you a thank you," Cain mumbled after a beat.

The entity chuckled. "Soon you will owe me much more than that. Get some rest. You will need it."

Cain watched as the entity disappeared into the ethers, as he rested against the cold, hard slab of granite. The center of his chest, where Aklia's blade pierced, pulsed with a new wave of pain. The silver still coursed its way through his veins, slowing down the healing process. He grimaced and forced his mind to focus on anything else but the pain. His thoughts drifted to Eliana, his second youngest daughter and his most fearless.

How long had it been since they had contact? He'd only heard bits and pieces about her, such as her "going mad," and creating an army of blood drinkers in a single night. He heard that she killed a king who was known for his cruelty against women, especially his wife. His Eliana had always exuded a soft spot for the female species, which on some level, he respected. He remembered the earlier days of her life when she longed to join the human tribes and live as they did. But within the last few years, he heard about her change. She killed for pleasure now. And with humanity undergoing a new genesis, he wondered just how they would continue when their baser natures had been indulged heavily. There was no running from who and what they were, and it would not be long before the archangels would hunt for them again.

But he would have plenty of time to figure this and many other things out. The earth had been flooded and there was no telling when the wrath of the sea would end. Until then, he would rest on this granite slab, picture those moments when Luluwa would lay her head on his chest, and hum the tune their mother would sing by the river. Memories were all that he had at this point, and no one would take them away.

***

40 days and 40 nights later…

This had been the longest stretch Cain and his family had endured without blood, but the entity had been true to his word that as long as they remained in the dark depths of the sub terrain, they would feel no thirst. Their bodies would not desire to be fed, and they would suffer no repercussions for the starvation. It was there, in the twisted shadows of the underworld that Cain learned many truths, including those that had been secreted away in the heavens. And it was there he felt more like himself. It was there that he discovered more of his power, his ability to manipulate the shadows, and enter the world of dreams to bring torment to his victims. He could not wait for the day when he set could foot topside.

But one question haunted the dark crevices of his mind, had Aklia's children survived?

The world had been reset, the goal having been to restore some balance and order to the chaos and destruction that threatened life itself.

Except for him.

Eliana watched her father from the large stone on which she sat. Selene, now equal in age to a human child of eleven years of age, curled up next to her, resting fitfully in her lap. She studied her sister's features, appreciating her full mouth, rich brown skin, and head full of thick, black hair that refused to remain braided. Her hair represented the wild untamed spirit that was Selene. So many years had passed before reuniting with what was left of her family. Her mother's death still tore at her soul. She wept for days on end when she learned the truth. Aklia deserved a far harsher death than what any of them could have imagined. The only solace she could find was in the serene expression in Selene's face. Out of all of them, Selene looked more like Luluwa,which made her feel as if her mother would always be with her.

"I miss her more than you understand," Cain said in the darkness. "She was the moonlight of my soul." His voice trailed off and both retreated into silence.

Nunka sat with his back against the wall, his head low, lost in his own thoughts. Cain had contemplated putting him out of his misery, being that his leg never regenerated. For as long as he lived, he would hobble and hop around with a stump. Anger ate away at Nunka.

"We will rebuild," Cain promised, studying his children, unsure of how dark of a turn their minds made.

"I know we will." Eliana exhaled. "We always do."

"And the humans will pay for what was done to us," Nunka vowed through exposed fangs.

"In time," Cain said calmly. "But first we rebuild."

Nunka said nothing. His vacant eyes remained fixed on where his right leg should have been.

Cain released another calming breath and retreated into his thoughts. It would be several hundred years before he could position himself to his full glory. As far as he knew, his name had been washed away with the rest of the sins of the world. And when the earth dried up, it was decided that they remain beneath the surface. The human population had been reduced to almost Adam and Eve proportions, which meant that their food source needed time to replenish itself before any of them stepped foot back into the world.

But when he returned, the same world that set out to destroy him, would be the very world that would beg for his mercy.

Chapter Twenty – Five

A thousand years later

Centuries after his return to the surface, humanity's battle with the ever present theme of good versus evil continued. Humans murdered their own kind for sport, for pleasure, and for revenge. Humans dominated other humans in a wicked game of chess, all in a quest for power. Humans, some of them vampiric in nature instead of bite, preyed on the weak, but still, there were those who clung to the light and held onto falsities such as hope and love. Upon his return to the surface, Cain sorted through the many tribes of humanity that eventually turned into civilizations, all in search of any signs of Aklia's bloodline; any human with extraordinary abilities, sheer strength, and a will to be matched. For those he came across, he made sure to eradicate the entire bloodline, therefore rendering many tribes lost. His children also became that of legend, striking fear into the hearts of their prey and once again in history, his name was uttered with terror.

And it would appear that this time, even the archangels had retreated to the heavens, abandoning the world to his will, and his will alone. Monuments were built in his name, and only the select few were awarded his bite to further his agenda and to protect his name. The name of the man he thought was his father was erased from the libraries, or at least buried far beneath his view.

Seated in a chair carved in marble high up on the temple mount, he observed his enslaved humans work night and day to build a step pyramid in honor of his fallen wife, Luluwa. If only she could see him now.

Selene, now at full maturity and a seasoned hunter, had taken refuge in the southernmost part of their growing kingdom, closest to the Nile. Out of all of his children, she had been the wildest, the most untamed, and the one who had stolen his heart. He had hoped to find a worthy human to turn into a suitable mate for her, but she declined, never tiring of her endless bounty of selected suitors. Eliana had taken up arms, her focus on defending their kingdom and nothing more.

Cain's thoughts drifted to his one-legged son, Nunka. Another female had been selected and turned into his bride, and now the male was preparing to add two more. The families of the girls being considered desired rank and whatever amount of power Cain would offer them.

He yawned at the thought. For all he cared, Nunka could cast them out to the fields to serve as laborers. The things humans would do to ensure their own survival, even if it meant sacrificing their own children, never really surprised him. Stroking away at his long beard, he continued to watch the humans struggle to lift the heavy stone blocks at the commands of the drivers, not paying attention to the fact that his son had materialized into physical form next to him.

"I think I've found the one for me father." Nunka smiled.

Cain sighed. "What do you mean? You have a wife that has been loyal to you for the last hundred years and two more that are being prepared. Now you mean to tell that you've found another one? How remarkable could she be that you are willing to forsake your current wife and brides to be?"

"Oh, please Father! You wouldn't make such comments if you could've seen her in action," Nunka grinned, his eyes lit with a slight crimson and his smile so wide his fangs stood out proudly on display.

Cain's expression became grim. "Seen her in action? What did she do?"

"She is not ordinary, Father, " Nunka said quickly. "But before you cast judgement, you should see her for yourself. She is absolutely divine!"

"Is she aware of your affections, Nunka? I shall not have my son fall victim to unrequited love."

"She is quite young and is not of marriable age as of yet," Nunka admitted.

"And so how do you know that she is the one?"

"Because when I saw her a few days ago in the square with her family, I noticed that her parents carried themselves with the spirit of the warrior. They acknowledged me and my men briefly, but their eyes held no fear, and when the child's gaze fell upon me, she was unafraid. It was as if she knew me, but in a way that no wife I could ever have could…"

"I still do not understand how a child could have that effect on you, son." Cain regarded him smugly. "Who is she? Who is her family?"

"She comes from a tribe of nomads, they stop only for food and rest, and from what I gathered, they were only passing through."

"And you let them?"

[133]

"I demanded that they stay and pay respect to our king and lord," Nunka replied evenly.

"And what came of it?"

"They said they were leaving come sunrise, but they would be sure to pay their respects to you before they left."

Cain frowned. "Nomads are not welcomed here. Bring me the girl so I can see what is so special about her."

Nunka nodded, his smile having disappeared at his father's request.

"You would be wise to mind the trespassers who frequent our gates. I may be ruler with a reputation for death and blood, but there are still other kingdoms rising, protected by forces we cannot name. Enemies will rise again, Nunka. Even the wise king to the north with his hanging gardens is a potential threat. Now go. Bring the girl and her family to me."

***

Cain's growl could be heard for miles as he surveyed the damage left by the girl's family. His suspicions had been correct, and he wondered if his son's sanity was stripped the moment, he lost his leg. How could Nunka not have known? Piles of ash rested on the steps and entryways of his main temples. Eliana had dispatched guards to search for the family that dared to smite him. The deaths of his sentinels registered in his senses before daybreak as he was speaking to a group of servants regarding a domestic matter.

Nunka was supposed to have retrieved the girl.

Images of the carnage filtered into his psyche. There were seven of them: four men and three women. They moved with coordinated accuracy, striking their opponents with the swiftness of a cobra. He remembered this all too well. Silver. Their weapons were all forged from silver. How? The flood had completely wiped the world of nearly every human available, and yet here they were.

"Nunka!" He bellowed through the halls, furiously bypassing another large pile of ash. Where was his foolish son?

His temple palace fell into an uproar as he placed a telepathic call to arms, sending images of the attackers to his guards and his children. Nunka's wife appeared before him, her big, Bedouin eyes wide with panic.

"I can't find Nunka anywhere," she whimpered. "I do not sense him, either."

Fury held Cain in its grip. His son's death had not registered as of yet, but it was quite odd that he could not be found.

"Keep searching for him," Cain commanded as he deconstructed into mist. "Find the attackers and bring me their heads!"

He allowed the airwaves to lift him and carry him around the perimeter of his palace until he reached the far end, towards the main exit, where seven warriors surrounded Nunka.

Nunka held the child in his grip and even still, the child possessed no fear. Her brown eyes held a familiar strength,

[135]

her honey brown skin crackled with unspent rage. Quickly, he threw himself into his physical form, his fangs on full display. And just as he reached for the closest warrior, a dark-haired female with even darker skin, surrounded by a bright light appeared, striking him down. Out of the bright light came none other than the person he believed he would never see again in any lifetime.

Aklia.

Her ghastly form gripped her blade as she stood face to face with her brother. For a second, he stood in disbelief. How? How was this possible?

"Attack!" she commanded the seven warriors behind her.

"This cannot be," Cain hissed as he dodged Aklia's swing.

"Oh, but it is," his sister spat.

He deconstructed into mist as she pivoted backwards and lunged towards him.

"Nunka!" Cain called out just as he witnessed his son throw the child, only for one of her protectors to catch her before she slammed into the wall.

Nunka, clearly unable to engage in battle on one leg, attempted to shift into a wolfen form, but with his disability, he could not shift fast enough to avoid the battle ax that pierced his spine or the spear that was shot into his neck. Cain watched as another one of his children, his only son disintegrated into ash.

"Nunka!" Cain bellowed, returning to his physical form. His son's death boiled in his blood, darkening the atmosphere around him. Eliana appeared behind him, armed with two short blades and several of her guardsmen.

Not wanting to risk another one of children, with the sheer force of his will, he sent out a shockwave that blew Eliana and her men backwards, crashing through the stoned wall and out into the yard.

"This is the last time you will ever take anyone from me again, Aklia!" Cain exploded.

Time shifted into a standstill as Cain reached for a nearby fighter, a giant of a male with a deep scar on his face. With his mind, he yanked the male towards him, prepared to snatch his beating heart from his chest., when a blast of bright light both blinded and burned his flesh.

"Demon be gone!" a voice boomed from the light.

"Until we meet again, brother," his sister said as she folded away into the light, along with the group of seven warriors and the child.

Cain rolled onto his side with a hard groan. His blood leaked onto the floor; pain radiating throughout his body. He knew that the room stank of singed flesh, but the numbness of his face prevented him from detecting it. His skin tingled as it began the process of repairing itself, but in the moment, none of that mattered.

His son was gone.

Nunka had yet to bring forth an heir, which had sparked many questions regarding fertility amongst his kind. He had hoped at some point his son would produce an heir with one of his wives, but as Fate would have it, it was just not meant to be. And now, what remained were his two daughters and a kingdom that would soon be under attack.

Those warriors fought much like his sister and it was evident that this special group of fighters were indeed connected to her. They possessed some of her strength and speed, but that child, there was something quite different about that child. To have angelic protection and Aklia as her guardian, Cain realized that Aklia's bloodline was never lost in the flood. Aklia's legacy as a Hwould continue and as Cain would discover, that child was only the precursor to much more to come.

Chapter Twenty – Six

"Part of winning the war is understanding your enemy," the entity whispered before materializing into his dark, shadowy form. "Your arrogance is what blinds you."

"What do you want?" Cain snapped, gently rubbing his face.

"I want to help you," the entity replied.

"You've done enough of that already," Cain grumbled.

"I would think you would display a little more gratitude, considering you were attacked with angel fire when your dear sister launched her surprise attack.. The reason why you are still standing is because of my blood."

Cain said nothing as he looked out of the window from high above in his temple. He had demanded height from his human slaves as a demonstration of his power. Plus, from this position, he would be able to see intruders from miles away.

"Your sister's blood lives," the entity continued. "I believed all of it had been washed away in the flood, but it appears there is something greater at stake here."

"I watched her die and yet she lives," Cain seethed. "How is that possible?"

"Her spirit ascended, having already mastered what it needed in order to do so. She fights on the side of the Archangels now."

"She will be an even greater problem dead than when she was alive," Cain murmured.

"More reason to explore why that is." The entity smiled. "I've been doing some studying of my own, observing the highs and lows, strengths and weaknesses, physical and spiritual aspects of humanity. Vessels, that's all they are. A means to carry out whatever agenda they are programmed for."

"What are you talking about?" Cain asked, curiously.

"Every single individual human born was designed for a specific purpose. Most of them will never fulfill that duty and therefore will return to the flesh after death until the assignment is completed. There are those born who are aware of their soul's purpose, much like your sister Aklia, and those who are born to be nothing more than pawns or cannon fodder. There are things that were spoken long before you were ever a conceivable thought; words that were spoken that are already coming to fruition.

This, everything you see, experience, remember, hear, taste and touch, is all part of a system of events geared towards a specific outcome. Your birth is of no consequence, just as the meeting of your mother and I in the Garden was a mere coincidence. All of this was allowed. You are who you are because it is *allowed*." The entity paused and took in a deep breath before continuing. "You are the key to the end, just as I was the key that unlocked the beginning. Think about it."

Cain's frown deepened as he focused on the mysterious form that stood before him. His thoughts drifted to his childhood. Could everything that transpired have been divinely orchestrated? What kind of sick game was this? Why was he chosen to be the thing, the monster, the demon as he was called, the first of his kind to walk the earth, filling the void between the living and the dead? How was it that his brother Abel was graced with the gift of living freely as he was without harm or judgement?

"Your soul knew. That's why you resented him so much," the entity whispered. "That's why you killed him."

Cain turned away, his eyes burning from the memory. "All I wanted was to live. To be normal."

"You did."

"I deserved to be loved just as much as Abel," Cain growled.

"You did."

"I did not ask to be born what I am."

"As none of us do – even those of us who were not technically born."

"Because of you and my mother's treachery, I had to suffer!" Cain roared as he slammed his fist into the wall, leaving a small crater behind.

"It is through me that your mother learned the truth and grew wise in many things." The entity grinned, unfazed by Cain's outburst. "I satisfied many of her curiosities. But be that as it may, let not your anger consume you. Adam is dead and you are not. Eve is dead and still you stand. You are older than the oldest human, stronger than any man or beast, faster with control over elements that humans could ever imagine."

"Why?" Cain demanded. "Since the beginning I have had nothing, and the little I did have was taken from me. What cosmic sin did my soul commit long before I arrived in the flesh?"

The entity opened his mouth to speak but found himself at a loss for words. Cain's eyes slowly normalized to their original brown color as he slouched on the marble bench that overlooked the window.

"You were a cosmic loophole that not even the Seraphim could have predicted," the entity continued after a beat. "Your creation has sparked a turn of events and manifested many a prophecy for the future that is yet to unfold. You serve as the ultimate reversal of humanity and the perfect weapon for the war that I've been preparing for since my introduction to Eden."

"And how exactly did my sister fit into all of this?"

"For every action there is a reaction or some sort of equal response to bring the universe into balance. Both of you are children of Eve and it was through Eve that you are standing here. Aklia was chosen to offset the damage and darkness that you unfortunately bring. And because you possess the capability to replicate extensions of yourself, if not through siring but through bite, Aklia' line must continue. It is much clearer now."

"What are you saying? That all of this was meant to be? That my pain is part of some divine plan?"

The entity shrugged. "Perhaps. As above so below. We all have a role to play in this war. Before I was cast out, I stumbled across a particular group of stars beyond the Gates of Orion. The Fire Bird, the protector and executioner of worlds known and unknown spoke of something yet to come. A Destroyer of some sort, the Light's greatest weapon would come and 'slay the dragon' but this Destroyer would only appear at the world's end. We are still at the beginning."

"I do not have time for these riddles!" Cain barked. "Nor do I care about this 'destroyer'! What I care about is how my sister still lives!"

"It would be wise of you to care," the entity replied. "Your sister lives because there is more to come. There will be others like her, yet to be born as her bloodline is the response to yours. I have much to learn, as all has yet to be revealed and I am banned from accessing the Books of Light, the Akashic Records. However, when there is a will there is a way. Remain in your misery if you must, but your ignorance is what has deepened your debt to me. "

And with, that the entity folded away into the shadows, leaving Cain alone to face his emptiness, his rage, and his grief. His sister lived and it appeared that another like her had been born underneath his nose. He would find the child and kill her before she could even pick up a sword, and those that followed her would meet their demise too. He would put an end to the games and that would fuel his desire to create a world that would belong to him and him alone.

***

"Nunka's death will not be in vain, Father," Eliana swore as a single tear slid down her cheek. "The humans will know no pain like that of which I will inflict."

"Nunka was a fool," Selene began as she sauntered toward her sister and Father from across the hall.

"You will watch your words, sister," Eliana hissed, exposing a perfect set of dagger like fangs.

"But he was," Selene continued with a yawn. "Ogling after a child? That was bound to bring some sort of retribution. He was the reason why that particular tribe breeched our walls."

"How many times must I warn you?" Eliana growled, her eyes flashing a deep red.

Selene idly pushed her wild mane away from her face and placed her hand on her round hip. "I love my brother. But I warned him about his activities. His brides were getting younger and younger and the humans were growing restless."

"That still does not explain how he is to blame for his own death!" Eliana exploded.

"Oh, but it does," Selene said, disregarding her sister and approaching her silent father. "He traveled the winds to the borders of the sea in search of new wife to replace Naima and found no one. None as ruthless and fearless as she

[143]

was. I remember the stories he spoke of her. He slaughtered whole villages, gorged himself on the blood of young women, and because of his carelessness, he tracked those warriors right to us."

"I will find them and show them no mercy!" Eliana seethed.

"I find it interesting that we had no idea that such a tribe existed. The lands of Adam are nothing but desert now. No life sprouts from those dry, infertile lands," Selene said thoughtfully. "I have traveled to the mountains and beyond and never witnessed anything of the such."

"They are protected by warrior angels and my sister, Aklia," Cain said finally. "Wherever they are, they are shielded from our detection."

"We can send humans to track them, learn their whereabouts, their strengths and weaknesses," Eliana said, her gaze searching her father's for approval.

"We can send our best men to search for them," Selene added. "We will have them infiltrate their land, and once we've learned everything about them…"

"We strike." Eliana and Selene shared a grin while their father sat stoically, contemplating their plan.

He continued to listen as his remaining children rattled on with a plan that held its weight in merit, but there was so much more they were missing. His thoughts drifted to the conversation he had with The Fallen, realizing that he too missed the mark when it came to understanding the system of things. His existence went beyond leaving a permanent scar on the world and reshaping it to his image.

He was a weapon in a war that humans had no idea they were fighting. The possibility of an even greater scheme, that was more than simply infiltrating the ranks of the enemy camp -but their minds made him smile. Angels could not go against free will and it would be free will that he would use to his advantage.

Part IV

The Seven

Chapter Twenty- Seven

"What are they, baba?" Nairobi asked her father as she watched the warriors drag a snarling young man with bloodshot eyes across the sand.

"Blood drinkers," he answered sternly. "Vermin."

The two warriors tossed the struggling creature before the puzzled Nairobi. The warm rays of the sun crept along the horizon, causing the entity's scream to reach ear drum shattering decibels. The entity scrambled and thrashed about on the dry desert sand, its blood red eyes meeting her gaze before reaching for her. Her father ZaNum kicked the creature in the face and both watched it roll over onto its stomach, struggling to push itself up.

"There are more of them," said the warrior, with a deep scar that ran deep across his broad chest. "We took out several and rescued a few villagers who are seeking shelter with our tribe."

"We cannot afford more refugees," Nairobi's father began. "Food is not the problem P'Tah, but we are slowly creating a trail that leads directly to us. We took out The Original's son."

"Good," P'Tah spat, glaring at the struggling creature. "There are three of them left, yes?"

"Yes. But Nunka as he was called," Nairobi's father continued. "Hunted Nairobi. He sought her out."

Nairobi looked down as concerned glances shifted in her direction.

"She is Chosen," P'Tah said after a beat. "These lands are protected. Blood drinkers and other demons cannot cross here."

"But they can try to force us out."

"Asuar," P'Tah said, meeting the warrior's hard stare. "We will protect, Nairobi. We have the word from the Heavens that she will be safe."

Asuar looked at his daughter, his heart swelling with both love and fear, the conflict between the two emotions warring with each other as memories of his wife resurfaced. Yasmine wielded her blade like the best of them, fought against their strongest opponents and still, the bite of their main enemy claimed her.

"It will not be the same for Nairobi," P'Tah promised. "Things will be different. *She* is different."

Without another word, Asuar reached into his waistband and pulled out a silver tipped short blade and handed it to Nairobi.

Nairobi looked up at him, eyes wide with confusion as her small, shaky hand accepted the weapon. Instinct slowly crept into her awareness as she glanced over at the creature that hissed in her direction.

"Your training begins today little one," Asuar informed her. "As does your legacy."

Nairobi gripped the weapon tightly in her palm. The creature swiped at her, barely missing her face. P'Tah snatched the creature by the back of the neck and flipped it on its back. Thick saliva and blood oozed from its fangs as another scream escaped from its mouth. Nairobi sucked in a steady breath. She'd seen this done many times by her father and the other members of her tribe. Closing her eyes, she released a battle cry of her own and lunged forward, plunging the blade deep into the entity's chest. Instantly, the creature's screams were cut off as it incinerated into dust on contact with the blade. Ash and sulfur filled the air and entered into Nairobi's airways. She coughed and gagged, but both P'Tah and her father gazed down at her with pride.

"Well done Nairobi." Asuar beamed. "Well done."

***

10 years later...

"It is said that Nairobi will go out on her first hunt," Selene murmured as she entered her father's chambers. Wrapped in his arms was his latest victim, a servant girl, struggling to win a losing battle against the vice like grip of an apex predator. Selene smiled as she watched her father slowly retract his fangs from the girl's throat.

"Aklia will be present then," Cain murmured, allowing the girl's body to fall on the floor. "That tribe has been a problem since Nunka's discovery of the Huntress."

"Which is why revenge was found in the death of her father, Asuar." Selene smiled. "As I recall, the mighty Asuar turned into the very thing he hunted, clawed his way up through the dirt in which his people buried him in, waited until dawn and allowed the sun to claim his final death."

"How poetic." Cain sighed. "I remember that all too well. And that also means that Nairobi will hunt with the vengeance of her ancestor. This story is bound to repeat itself."

"Eliana and her guards will be patrolling the fields tonight," Selene continued. "I too will keep watch."

"There is something I must do," Cain began, taking a stand. "In studying this new Huntress, I realized my error in choosing to remain ignorant."

"What do you mean?"

"Years ago, I was warned to look a little deeper into the existence of myself and Aklia. Aklia and all of her children are of flesh and blood, but capable of inhuman feats, immune to our infection, masters of the elements, but also skilled warriors. As a matter of fact, Aklia and her children have always held the favor of the Archangels despite her blood being tainted with that of Adam's. They can die but are harder to kill."

"I've always wondered how and why," Selene added. "I supposed that just as in all things, there are opposites: light and dark, hot and cold, fire and ice, human and blood drinker. Nature always balances itself out and perhaps we are the balance to humanity and Aklia has been the balance to us."

Cain stopped to gaze at his beautiful daughter. Selene reminded him so much of his lost Luluwa, it unnerved him. Her beauty seemed to be never ending with her emerald green eyes, high cheek bones, and perfectly sculpted, heart shaped face. Her dark hair hung loosely in thick curls past her shoulders like her sister Eliana. Eliana possessed a more delicate appearance, soft plush lips on a round face, with large slanted eyes on a tight, lithe body. Tati had been a more savage form of beauty with wild locks and fiery eyes with a personality to match. But Selene held the beauty of the moon, hence her name. Her suitors were endless and those who earned both her affection and her favor were granted the opportunity for life eternal as a blood drinker.

His beautiful Selene, his Luluwa incarnate.

"Whatever the case may be, I need answers. There is a seer just east of here. The locals say she has great power and I need to see it for myself."

"The locals believe just about anything." Selene sneered. "I've heard of this woman too and if her power is as great as they say, please be careful."

Cain looked at his daughter, admiring the detailed design of the silk robing that covered her every curve. The image of Luluwa's face came to mind, which he quickly brushed off.

"I will. Give me a full report on Nairobi's hunt. Soon, it will be time for the young Huntress and I to have a formal introduction."

Chapter Twenty – Eight

The journey to the Seer, the gifted human with the ability to see and walk in between the Veil of Life and Death, amounted to a two and a half day's walk. But for Cain, the journey was but a few minutes. Isolated and tucked away within the bush, her tiny dwelling was made of mud brick and thatch, so Cain materialized with caution. Despite the humble appearance, he had learned long ago of what gifted humans were capable of defensively. Magic and powerful curses had worked against his kind effectively, and for all he knew, this could easily be a set up.

"I knew you would come, blood drinker," came a soft voice from the bush. "Stay right where you are. You do not have permission to cross into my home."

He froze. Confused, he tried to press closer to the small hut, only to find himself blocked by an invisible barrier.

"How do you do this?" he demanded.

"That is not of your concern," said the voice.

"Show yourself," Cain commanded. "I do not wish to harm you. I just need answers."

"You do not wish to harm me, but you harm many others," the voice retorted. "What is the difference?"

"I survive just as any other being on this planet," Cain grumbled.

"You are not a being, but a curse."

Her comment gave him pause. "I am what I am. I did not ask for any of it."

"True enough."

"Show yourself," Cain commanded once more.

"I do not respond to the demands of demons," she retorted. "But I will tell you what you want to know."

"The Prophecy," Cain said quickly. "My sister. Her descendants…"

She appeared almost instantly, revealing her haggardly hunched form. Bright blue eyes stared back at him from a wrinkled face. Her sun kissed, leathery skin, made from too much time spent under the sun, was barely covered by the dingy rags she wore for clothing. Straight white hair hung loosely down her spine. She looked at him with contempt and Cain wondered just how great her power truly was. To him, she looked like nothing more than an old bag of dust. But judging from their few moments of engagement, he received the sense that she would make a great adversary.

"The Heavens had predicted that a Darkness would inhabit this earth after the war; and this Darkness would presume for many lifetimes to come. You carry the blood of that Darkness, a Fallen, and perhaps one of the strongest Fallen to have ever been created. Deception happened in the Garden, thus setting forth a series of irrevocable events that will be corrected. Your sister is the beginning. Your kind will wage war with her offspring, who are protected by the Divine."

"Yes, yes, I know but get on with it," Cain complained. "What is The Prophecy?"

"Foolish Son of Darkness, there are many prophecies, but I can only give you one," the woman snapped.

[153]

"For it is foretold the Beast should bear an heir and the world would drown in blood. First born carries the Curse and with this Curse the earth will flood. Her sword is fierce and true, molded by fire and blessed by the Archangels. She carries the Light of the Sun and the Truth from the Heavens to restore what is lost. In the final hours, when the war between the Brothers of Light and the Brothers of Dark finds its way to earth, she will be called to lead. She is not the first but the last for it was her first mother who paved the path. Protectors, the Sons and Daughters of Seth will act as her guide, possessing gifts from the Heavens, this Huntress – for her they will fight. For this dark curse will roam the earth to and fro, and into the bowels of Hell he will go... for another heir will assume dominion once the curse is past until the final battle between what was first and what was last."

The old woman looked at him and smiled, revealing a snaggle tooth. "Enjoy your time on this earth while you may, for what is coming, is here to slay." Her cackle rippled through Cain as she disappeared in a puff of smoke.

Cain spun around searching for her, but could not detect her presence, "Deranged witch," Cain spat. He took a hard step toward her house but bumped right into the invisible barrier.

"I will have your head, witch!" Cain bellowed. "You spill nothing but lies!"

The only response Cain received was the gentle push of the wind. With a frustrated sigh, Cain disappeared into the ethers. Selene reported that Nairobi's first hunt would begin that eve and it would only be fitting that he was present to formally introduce himself.

Chapter Twenty- Nine

"Your father would have been proud to see you wield Aklia's sword," P'Tah told her as she sheathed the weapon on her hip.

"I know. We are going to take down as many blood drinkers as we can," Nairobi said, her eyes focused on the ground.

"You will. You have proven yourself countless times." P'Tah smiled confidently.

Nairobi's eyes narrowed as a snapshot images of her father from unforgotten memories she kept tucked away resurfaced. "I will avenge my father," Nairobi swore. "I will fight until my last dying breath to see to it that those demons are nothing but ash."

P'Tah stood quietly as Nairobi marched off towards the chosen warriors who would fight alongside Nairobi on her journey as a Huntress. Aklia had personally selected the group of seven fighters: three women and four men. Nairobi's legacy as the huntress, will be the first in over a thousand years to stand against the blood drinkers that haunted the world. Her dark hair, woven into dozens of intricate braids, hung below her waist like rope. Her even darker eyes held a quiet fury that burned with the brightness of the flames that kept them warm at night.

Their tribe had grown into a small nation, broken into several sects in which P'Tah ruled. Asuar had been his most trusted fighter and when it was revealed that this special Huntress had been born of Asuar's blood, P'Tah appointed Asuar as chief of what was known as The Chosen's sect. And to demonstrate the strength of their bond, it was agreed that Nairobi, would marry P'Tah's youngest son when she did come of age but once Nairobi first picked up Aklia's blade, P'Tah knew that things would be different. She was a warrior. Blood and war burned in her veins while the universe called out to her to fulfill her destiny. A destiny that he would soon accept did not include him or his son.

"I can sense them moving towards the village near the spring," Nairobi announced. "Let's move!"

War horns blasted throughout the kingdom. Children ran with their families into their homes as the gates prepared to make way for Nairobi and her warriors. Darkness crept along the edges of the last remaining rays of light. P'Tah looked on as Nairobi mounted her Kamal, her camel, and prepared to take off to face the enemy.

P'Tah wished that he possessed the gifts that Asuar's daughter held; with them, he could have protected his people better. Asuar and his cluster of people had wandered the deserts before crossing paths with P'Tah. The two tribes had nearly gone to war because P'Tah believed that they were practitioners of dark arts. Asuar, in particular proved himself to not only be an extraordinary fighter, but capable of moving and manipulating matter with his mind. P'Tah's wisdom encouraged him to view Asuar as an asset, something that he never regretted. When the blood drinkers first appeared, it was Asuar and his warriors who fought them off and soon after, they were welcomed into the kingdom.

And now Nairobi carried the torch that her father left behind. But she was something stronger. Faster. And she held the gift of sensing the enemy, which gave them all the advantage. P'Tah promised Asuar that he would care for Nairobi as if she were his own should he fall, and when he did, P'Tah honored every word.

"Be careful, little one," P'Tah murmured under his breath as she took off. "Guards! Close the gates! Prepare for entry!" he shouted toward the giant sentinels that guarded the gates.

***

Cain smiled in the darkness as the death of another one of his night creatures disintegrated into ash. Nairobi had taken down three so far that hunted the small tribe of innocents who camped near the Euphrates. He could have called them back to him before she leveled her blade against them, but he needed to test her strength. Would she be as good of an adversary as his sister Aklia? Hidden just a few miles north of where she hunted, beyond the scope of detection, he watched her from the ethers. Her warriors were just as ruthless as the ones that he first encountered on that fateful eve of Nunka's death. The chime of the blade cutting through the nothingness had the same ring as Aklia's, reminding him of that fateful morning when her blade left her grip and struck the target in his chest.

"She is strong," Eliana whispered as she took form on the hilltop. "I've already sent scouts to the gates of P'Tah. While she is fighting, we could attack. That would send a message to her."

"Good. Send more to surround the gates. Once she returns to defend her people, I will strike. We will end this. For good," Cain vowed between his teeth.

Eliana nodded before disappearing into the airwaves. Nairobi's war cries echoed into the distance, music to his ears. And then the scent, the smell of her blood reached his nostrils even without him remaining in physical form. The phantom taste of her reminded him of honey and milk. How he suddenly wished he could bathe in the magic that was her. What was that? The response in his loins forced into physical form as the need to mate increased. It had been so long since he satisfied the thirst of his loins – no female could ever compare to his Luluwa. Sex could never be the same nor hold the same value as it once did. But the scent in the air thickened, tightening his groin. Images of Nairobi flooded his mind. Her hatred became his as her sword came down on another blood drinker. Her fury tainted the air. Her heartbeat became the rhythm of war. Her skin dripped with her sweat as she mounted her camel to ride off after another blood drinker that tried to escape.

The urge to go to her paralyzed his thoughts. And just as the temptation to surrender to his baser desires took hold, Selene appeared in front of him.

"Father, Eliana is ready," she said quickly, stopping short to survey him. "Is everything alright?"

"Everything is fine," Cain snapped. "Go. I will be right behind you."

She offered him an amused grin. "By the end of the night, you should celebrate with a female."

Cain glared at her before she disappeared into mist. He forced himself to refocus on the task at hand. He kept his mind on Nairobi's energy signature. She must've picked up on the danger that approached her people as she made a hard turn back towards the kingdom.

He dematerialized and took to the airwaves. When all of this was done, he pondered on taking his daughter's advice. Just thinking about Nairobi's scent made his gumline thicken. Maybe her blood would quell the fire that burned in his veins as he pictured licking the sweat off of her neck. As he pressed forward, he looked forward to finding that out.

***

Nairobi and her warriors arrived in time to assist P'Tah's men fight the small army of blood drinkers that raided their territory. She had prepared for this fight for years and it had been her vision to end it. Her people deserved to live in peace without fear of what was to come when night fell.

She jumped off Kamal's back into a hard sprint, surprising the unsuspecting blood drinker by cutting off its head. Ash and sulfur filled the air. Innocents were dragged from their homes and more blood was spilled. She could hear P'Tah's grunts as he swung his blade while simultaneously dodging a hard swipe from talons. Her warrior and protector, Anu appeared from the shadows to flank P'Tah, and the two of them fought back to back.

A female materialized behind her, nearly towering over Nairobi's 5'0" frame. Her dark skin nearly blended in with the surrounding darkness, enhancing her menacing appearance. Crimson red stared back at Nairobi as she took on a fighting stance.

"I remember when you were but a child," Eliana hissed. "You stole from us then and you continue to steal from us as I speak. This comes to an end."

"All you leeches do is steal the lives of the innocent!" Nairobi declared as she lunged forward. "You are a disease! A curse!"

"We are what we are." Eliana punched Nairobi's, rattling her to the bone.

Nairobi quickly shook it off, returning with a series of kicks and punches that Eliana expertly blocked.

"You fight well," Eliana taunted. "But not good enough."

The connection between Nairobi's rage and the fire element was almost instant. Eliana made the mistake of reaching for the Huntress in a psychic snatch, that should have pulled out her still beating heart. But instead, Nairobi's body became lined with searing fire. Cain yanked his fangs from the neck of one of her warriors, and from across the open field, he watched as Nairobi incinerated Eliana with a blast of fire. The familiar embrace of grief shrouded him with pain that he couldn't escape. Not another one. Not another one of his children.

Tati. Tyre. Luluwa. Nunka. And now Eliana. This was his fault. He sanctioned this.

A pair of hands gently touched his shoulders, temporarily distracting him from his grief. It was Selene, his last and only surviving heir.

"We have to go," she urged. "I've pulled out the remaining blood drinkers. We will win this war, but not tonight."

He allowed his daughter to lead him out of the territory until they reached the border of the lands in which he called his own. Inhabitants had soon come to call this The Land of Cain. Humans had entered, but very few exited. His land had become an isolated terrain that only the bravest of the brave dared to venture. The remaining humans worshipped him as a god, and he used them to fulfill whatever purpose his kingdom needed.

"We will have our revenge," Selene swore to her father, who stared blankly to the horizon. "I promise you."

"And so," Cain murmured, still staring off into the distance. "It has begun."

Chapter Thirty

Nairobi had been the first Huntress born after the death of
Aklia and the disappearance of her living descendants after
the flood. Nairobi's legacy became the blueprint for the
next line of Huntresses to follow. The Sumerians called
these special fighters the *Akhkharu Alal* which, translated
to *Destroyer*. But just as the rise in the legend of the
Huntress made its way to developing cultures, so did the
mystery of the vampire. Despite all of Cain's attempts,
Nairobi lived to see the ripe old age of one ninety and even
then, she still proved herself capable of yielding her sword.
But just as the Light soon learned to diversify the Huntress
gene, Cain would follow suit. He would also learn that each
Huntress would evolve, increase in strength and will power,
each one becoming more difficult to kill. Unlike her
protectors who too possessed other worldly gifts, the
Huntress possessed an immunity to his bite, but even that
came with exceptions.

Exceptions that would indeed play to his favor.

Annalia was the first to succumb to his will through
seduction. The fiery Huntress rejected and abused her
Guardians, to Aklia's horror. Stronger than Nairobi, Cain
soon learned of her desire to rule rather than serve. Selene
had been the one to discover the huntress in the lands north
of the sun. And when the time came for Aklia to bestow her
sword during the coming of age ceremony, Aklia did not
appear as custom. To further add insult to injury, the young
slayer's Guardians abandoned her, leaving her to the
whispered promises of Cain.

Her soft pale skin carried the soft light of the moon, and her
long dark hair added a beautiful contrast to her rare form of

beauty. Her skills as a Huntress made her an invaluable addition to his developing plan of dominating humanity. However, when she rose the next morning as a mistress of the night, his ability to sire through her womb would soon be proven to be futile. Cain reasoned that perhaps in her human state, she had been born infertile.

But she would prove herself to be useful in many ways.

"You will have your crown and your glory, my beautiful queen of the night," Cain whispered as she mounted him.

She hissed as he filled her to capacity. A moan escaped her lips and he cupped her breasts. It had been too long since he indulged in the carnal pleasures of the flesh. Luluwa would always rest in his heart, but his body still needed to be fed in ways that did not include blood.

"Revenge on those who betrayed me will be crown and fulfilling the prophecy will be my glory," she murmured. Her cheeks still flushed with color as she rode him, the orgasm too close for her to stop. He gripped her waist as she picked up the pace, her thighs slamming hard onto his.

She would make a fine queen. If only she could give him heirs. Perhaps it was her Huntress gene that prevented him from siring from her womb, he contemplated. Or perhaps, in time his seed would be planted just as it had with Luluwa. But he didn't contemplate too deeply, and for a time, allowed Annalia to fill the void that Luluwa's death left in his heart. Together, the two of them struck fear in the hearts of even the bravest of humans who dared attempt to slay them.

And when the next Huntress came of age, Cain's plan of seduction worked tremendously. It seemed as if the Light had selected the wrong vessels to be off the greatest service to humanity. Kara was the next to join the fold, for Annalia had detected her presence in her old lands. Flaming red hair with emerald green eyes to match a spirit engulfed in pure wildfire, Cain could not resist the temptation that defined Kara. But just like Annalia, he would discover that an heir would not be possible with her.

The desire to sire, to create a new breed of vampire with all of the traits of the Huntress and none of the weaknesses, drove him to seek out the next generations of huntresses. Natasha, born of the Celtic clan of the north had been the next point of his obsession. Fierce with her bow and arrow, the brown eyed warrior successfully eradicated the increasing werewolf populations that threatened the survivability of her people. But her willpower was extraordinary. The first time she engaged with him in battle, she led a small team of Guardians directly to his lands, having tracked him to his lair.

Annalia was the first to attack, acting as his shield, and to see the two Huntresses engage in combat was like watching lightning strike. The hard chime of Aklia's blade sent Annalia into a frenzy that almost got her killed. She became reckless, furious, and determined to snatch the blade she felt was ill deserved from Natasha. Cain barely missed his head being severed from his shoulders when he reached for Annalia, and the two managed to escape to safety. It would be many battles such as this one before Natasha would ultimately be defeated in a fight to the death match against Annalia.

And even after Natasha's death, Cain still hoped to claim another Huntress.

Annalia, Kara, Kali, Helena, Muriel, Briya, and Tadaya became his Seven. And with them at his side for nearly a century, they razed the planet. And after the fall of Tadaya, no other Huntress would be born. The age of Kings had risen, humans had now surpassed tribal living, and the advancement of civilizations increased. Lessons remembered from the Fallen were incorporated into the daily lives of those who built the pyramids. Humans thought of themselves as gods or as descendants of gods, and it was then that these same humans looked to the heavens to aid in the slaying of their enemies.

One of their enemies being Cain.

He watched with amusement as the human servant girl scurried past him after changing the bedding in his chambers. Her family had committed her to a life of servitude after incurring a great deal of debt to him. In a rare act of mercy, in exchange for their exile rather than their lives, he requested the life of their youngest and most beautiful daughter, Amira. Despite her attempt to lessen her beauty by cutting off her locks, her baldness accentuated the perfect symmetry of her face, and highlighted the soft brown irises that peered out from her almond shaped eyes. Selene had been unnecessarily cruel to the young female, forcing her to partake in the most humiliating of tasks. But the girl demonstrated strength and resilience and fulfilled every last one of Selene's requests without complaint.

But those noble qualities of hers would not be enough to pay off the debt, and being that she was in service to living, breathing monsters, it would be in her best interest to use those qualities to her advantage if she was going to survive. For as long as she remained in service to his family, she would need more than a set of teeth and a pretty face if she wanted to see the sun.

The sun. When was the last time any of his children bore witness to the rays of light that provided both answer to the darkness and life itself? Selene was of his blood, born, not bitten, and the sun was never stripped from her existence. But his Seven? And the multitudes of other vampires that were bitten, if not by him, but his progeny?

"I thought I would find you here," Annalia's voice interrupted his thoughts as she sauntered into his chambers. "Why do you not join us for a hunt? I have learned that there is a group of travelers destined to cross the Tigris."

"It is best that we remain within our borders for now," Cain murmured, giving Annalia an appreciative once over. "Something tells me that we are being hunted."

"Oh, lover," Annalia cooed as she approached him slowly. The bright red robing that she wore clung to every curve of her slender form, and her hint of fang added to the dangerously intoxicating appearance of porcelain death. "The world now quivers beneath our feet. Rivers run blood rather than water because you will it so. Any enemy that dares to encroach upon us will face immediate retribution. We have nothing to fear."

She wrapped her cold arms around him and ran her tongue against his neck until it brushed against his ear lobe. "You worry too much," she told him.

"My instincts are what have kept me alive," Cain said, offering her a slight grin.

"And of course, my help," came the familiar voice of an entity from behind him as it took form. Annalia jumped back and hissed. The Fallen One laughed as Cain ushered himself in front of her.

"Go," Cain told her. "This is not of your concern."

Annalia glared at the entity before deconstructing herself into mist. Cain waited until she disappeared before speaking.

"She's obedient," The Fallen One stated. "I like that."

"What do you want?" Cain scowled.

"It's been centuries since I graced you with my presence," the entity replied evenly. "And I see that you took my advice. You managed to turn Seven of them. Interesting."

"Seven compared to the dozens that could not or I should say, would not bend to my will." Cain huffed.

"The point is that you used their Free Will against the Light. Nice work." The entity paused. "But not enough to beat the prophecy."

"Again, why are you here?" Cain demanded, growing annoyed with the entity's presence.

"I have been what you would call empire building," The Fallen declared. "Recruiting even. There is a new hierarchy that I have set in place, and because of you, I can move forward with my strategy."

"A strategy for what?"

"Well, your name is the beginning of the legacy that I promised you way back when. There is so much more at stake."

"So, you've been busy, " Cain added. "I am well aware of your more recent creations. Wolves beholden to the moon? Really?"

The entity chuckled. "That took quite a bit of working and blood spilling. I doubt there will be another Eve to assist me."

Cain cringed at the mention of his mother's name but said nothing.

"Be that as it may, as you can see, my time has been used wisely and effectively, unlike you and your seven concubines."

"I don't have time for this," Cain snarled.

"You may not have much time left, period. The Light is always working and moving. You took Seven of what was supposed to be the Light's ultimate weapons, and for that, there will be retribution. Instead of acting like an insolent child insistent upon getting his cock wet and ruling the world, I encourage you to accept my guidance, just as you accepted my help in the not so distant past."

When Cain said nothing, the entity continued. "The archangels have crossed the barrier into the physical world. They are coming for you, but more specifically, your concubines. You have been allowed to exist because of what is foretold to come, but your poor choices have led to another cosmic cleanse."

Cain contemplated the entity's words. But if the archangels hunted him, where would he hide? What stone could he cower under that would prevent his extermination? His vision of his future as sole ruler of this realm had yet to come fully into fruition, yet the price that he continued to pay did not equate to the possible gain.

"I have already created a world with a throne for you to sit," the entity offered.

"You mean, The Pit? Hell? I was born to take my place as the ruler of demons?" Cain spat, glaring at the entity in disbelief.

"Not exactly. What I offer you is command over an almost infinite army. I offer you real power."

"I already have power.'

"There will come a time, foolish one, when you will find yourself alone, cornered like a frightened animal, baying at the moon in your misery. There is a war that began long before you were the fruit of my loins and a war that I am determined to win. My blood is the reason why you even exist and because it is my blood that pumps through that black heart of yours, one day when I call, you will come."

"I doubt that day will ever come," Cain said evenly.

"Hmph." The entity snorted. "This will be my final warning of what is to come. Any assistance provided by me will be a debt owed."

Cain held the entity's dark gaze, but did not say anything.

"The archangels have crossed the barrier and are eradicating your kind as we speak. You violated cosmic law by creating the Seven, and for that, their souls are actually in my domain and I intend on using them to the fullest extent that I can. Their souls might even be one of the bargaining chips that will work in my favor. I would suggest that you disband your merry little group of bandits and seek refuge in the Sea of Three Points. At least there it will be more of a challenge to find you."

"If you are so great and powerful," Cain challenged. "Why don't you stop them? Why don't you bend them to your will?"

"Because this not a game of brute strength, nor is it a purpose of collecting casualties. This is a game of strategy and if you haven't figured it out by now, it is a game for the soul. Now, go!"

Chapter Thirty- One

In less than seven days, Cain would soon learn that The Fallen entity had been right in his warning. Four of the Seven – his special Huntresses – were taken out by the Light's Special Forces. Briya, Tadaya, Helena, and Muriel were killed by angelic blade. He had hoped to escort them out of the lands that he called home for many centuries. He could detect the energy of Aklia's signature written in all of this, and once he figured out a way to make her pay, she would pay dearly.

Selene had disappeared, refusing to follow him and his chosen. And thus, the reign of the Lands of Cain came to an end.

Their deaths registered in his blood, blotting out all of his senses as he and his last three fallen Huntresses made their way towards the Black Sea. A large ship rose with the tide as it sat docked on the port. A gathering of humans were too busy loading the vessel with goods to notice the appearance of Cain, Kali, Kara, and Annalia. The heat of the sun crept along the horizon and he could sense the energies of his females diminishing. If he did not act quickly, they would be ash.

Several orbs of bright light appeared just a few yards from where the closest human rested his barrel of goods. With his remaining energy reserves, he dematerialized all four of them and used his power to manipulate the wind to blow them onto the ship. They collapsed in full form in the hull. His three Huntresses scurried into hiding underneath the floorboards to protect themselves from the sun.

"Demon! We will smite you yet!" came the enraged voice of Michael.

"Does that mean you are willing to risk the souls of innocents?" Cain challenged.

"We will have your head demon one way or another, demon," Michael vowed. *"Even if we have to follow this ship until it ports."*

Cain growled in the darkness that consumed the bottom of the ship. He had no idea where the ship was destined, but he did know that it had to change its course. Manipulating the minds and will of humans was a gift that came with ease, but this feat would require more energy than usual. Once the ship set sail, determined upon its course, by then the humans would develop a sudden change of plans. With Michael and his archangels determined to trail after the ship to launch an attack once the ship docked, Cain could only hope that the Sea of Three Points in the south Atlantic would offer a safe refuge.

Provided the King of Liars did not lie.

But then again, the entity had been truthful thus far, provided that he had everything to gain.

"Cain," Annalia whispered weakly. "Where do you take us?"

"Somewhere safe. Rest. You all are safe."

***

For one hundred days the ship drifted from the Black Sea and into the Atlantic. The crew of seventy- five men and the few large families, which totaled out to be almost one hundred and fifty that paid to set sail along the coastal shores of the Black Sea, had nearly been reduced to sixty. Confusion and fear set in as many preferred to risk the

[172]

mercy of the sea than to face the terrors that waited when the sun set. Cain struggled to stave off the hunger of his three Huntresses by supplying them with his own blood. But being confined to such close proximity to humans, the scent of their blood and sweat gradually became too much even for him to ignore.

"Clean kills," he told them. "The food cannot become the hunter."

Night after night they fed and bled the ship until it was dry as it drifted farther out in the Atlantic. With no crew to guide her, Cain realized the mistake that they'd made. One night, after spending several nights without the hope of feeding, the urge to risk everything and swim to land was all too tempting.

"If we leave this boat," Annalia whispered to him. "The angels will pick us off one by one."

And that reminder alone kept Cain and his huntresses on the ship. By daybreak, after nearly two months of starvation, the ship found itself being pulled into the direction of a hard current. Winds had picked up and from the sky, Cain overheard the bellow of Michael as the energy of the Devil's Triangle pulled them into its epicenter. Relief claimed him as he peered out at the shoreline from the deck of the ship.

The ship docked a few hours later, thrusting itself upon a cluster of rocks several yards away from the sand. The crisp sound of the ocean waters crashing against each other brought him some peace while the seagulls above squawked their welcome from above. The three remaining Huntresses remained on board to hide from the sun, whose rays still burned brightly against the backdrop of the clear blue sky.

Stay here, he said to them mentally.

Ok, they collectively agreed. *We need humans.*

I know, he continued, shaking his head.

Sea salt tainted the air and entered his pallet. This was much different from the deserts and valleys and jungles that he been accustomed to. Here, the water were much more assertive in its command of the land, and in his line of vision, a cluster of trees with various species of fruits clinging to their branches stretched out for miles. He moved his bare feet in the sand and allowed the vibrations of the earth to flow through him. His nose detected the vague scent of human, but that of the tribal origin. A fire burned off in the distance – he could taste the smoke. Hunger ate away at his belly, but unlike his Huntresses, who could only sustain on blood, he could catch a few fish or even pick fruit off the tree to eat, which would give him enough strength to learn the layout of the new land.

And so it would be here that he, Cain, son of the Fallen, would begin again. The warrior angels would not be able to track him for many centuries and it would be here that he would fully learn how to use his power, to move in the shadows, to manipulate the elements to work in his favor, and also an appreciation for the delicate balance between predator and prey.

Part V

Chapter Thirty- Two

As it came to pass, the Curse of Cain trickled down into the hidden scrolls of human history. Once again, he managed to escape the wrath of even the Archangels after finding refuge within the Devil's Triangle. But as time went on, the priorities of the heavens shifted towards the greater cause of humanity: its salvation.

Over the years, Cain overheard tales of warrior women, some of them believed to have been birthed by the gods, acting as defenders of humanity while possessing gifts or talents that defied the laws of the supernatural. And as Cain would soon learn, the First of the Fallen had done exactly as he had promised. He managed to unleash the perverted spirits of the dead. Like a mad scientist hell bent on his own creations, the underbelly of the spirit world, which was once nothing more than a void, became the epicenter for the non-human. Some of his brethren – those who fled before and after the Flood – joined his ranks, thus forming their own organized hierarchy of chaos.

As above, so below.

And therefore, blood drinkers were not the only abominations that hunted the humans. Myths and legends involving demons who demanded the sacrificing of children, creatures of monstrous proportions that stalked the human populations had come to be, and as a result, those who served the heavens were forced to shift their focus. Human fear clung to the atmosphere like a thick blanket. Death, disease, and destruction plagued civilization after civilization, fattening humans with corruption like a pig in preparation for a dark feast.

His huntresses grew weary of the seclusion of the Devil's Triangle, and after several centuries of near death matches against each other, each decided to risk their lives for individual freedoms, with Kali being the first to leave. Kara followed the humans who migrated to the lands of the northern seas, seeking to return back to the land from which she came. She found solace with a tribe of wanderers who worshiped her, believing her to be a gift – a protector of sorts from the gods. Cain had wished them all well on their journeys, realizing that there was so much more at stake than holding them hostage to his company.

All of them except for Annalia.

Resentment had long permeated her dark heart as she did not feel fulfilled in her quest for vengeance. Annalia had envisioned leading her own army of turned huntresses in completion of her destiny as the strongest huntress ever born. At first Cain had long entertained such fantasy, amused with her vendetta against his sister, Aklia who no longer joined them in the physical realm. The huntress had rightfully felt cheated in her claim to victory when Aklia never appeared for her rites of passage as the next Huntress of her bloodline to hand her the blade that she once carried, the same blade that had pierced his own heart. Yet Cain had long been warned of the special Slayer that had yet to be born and he knew that Annalia was not The Chosen One.

Even still, after many centuries of loyalty and service, on the night before her decided departure, Cain opened his eyes to find a wooded spear trembling in her grip just above his heart. He smiled, fully knowing that it was all a ruse and simply part of her manipulative scheme to force him into moving forward with her demands.

"Is this where we are now?" He asked, unconcerned with the spear that hovered directly over his heart.

"You have made it so," she seethed through clenched teeth.

"Ah, I see." He studied the carefully and freshly carved spear. One hard push would be all that it would take to at silence him for a while. And he would hate to have to endure that again. "And what have I done to deserve this treachery?"

"You have taken so much from me, demanded so much from me, and have given me very little," she growled. Her midnight blue eyes burned a crimson red. Her pale skin seemed to glow underneath the moonlight, something that he loved about her. It was like she possessed her own version of moonlight in her skin, carrying the moon with her always.

"I believe that I have given you much," he said smoothly. "Immortality. Power. An opportunity to recreate your legacy…"

"You made me the thing that I was destined to hunt," Annalia seethed. "You turned me into a monster!"

"Then if you feel driving that stake into my heart, will do you some justice then please…" Cain relaxed, stretching out his arms to further expose his bare chest. "Do it. Give me your pain so that you may go on in peace."

Her trembling hand gripped the spear tighter, the wood digging into her own skin. Cain waited, watching patiently at the hard rise and fall of her chest. Her anger was deeper than any sea he could swim, darker than any night he would live, and it shone in the single tear that fell from her face. And then in a blink, the spear disappeared, and she was on her feet. Cain looked at her, disappointment weighing heavy in his heart and in his bones. Had she been another opponent, another anyone, he would have snatched her heart from her chest and thought nothing of it.

But this was his Annalia.

"I will take leave of you, Cain," she told him. "And one day, Aklia's blade will be in my grip and you will regret the day that you knew me."

"I will see you soon, Annalia," Cain said evenly. "Enjoy your freedom."

Annalia's frown deepened before she disappeared into the ether, taking leave into the breeze. Cain didn't blink once as the last traces of Annalia's scent disappeared. Her actions were not entirely surprising. He had detected her resentment towards him a while ago. Kali and Kara had been unquestioningly loyal, enduring the most difficult of times without complaint. Annalia on the other hand became more difficult to manage and as time went on, Kali and Kara became the focal points of her frustrations. Granting both Kali and Kara their freedoms had saved their lives, at least for now. All of them had targets on their backs by those in the heavens and even those below. But at least the curses brought upon humanity redirected angelic attentions, and as long as his Huntresses remembered everything, he taught them, they would survive. In time, he knew he would call on them again, but now it was best that they explore the world from their own perspectives.

The gentle crash of the waves against the seashore jarred him from his thoughts while simultaneously bringing forth the conclusion that it was time for a change. No more hiding. It was time for him to return to the epicenter of humanity and continue with his search for the prophesized huntress, - the slayer that Annalia had desperately wanted to be. He had already taken a blade to the heart once, and that wasn't enough to end him, so just how powerful would this huntress have to be to be mentioned in a prophecy? None of the Huntresses born since the death of Aklia had matched her strength or power, and he wondered just when he would have the pleasure of encountering such a creature.

Wherever you are, little huntress, Cain thought to himself as he became mist. *I will find you.*

Chapter Thirty – Three

4th Century A.D. Kingdom of Axum (Eritrea and Ethiopia)

"You mean to tell me that you were there in Golgotha when He broke bread and drank the wine, the night that he was turned over to the Pilate?" the young priest asked, his bright eyes filled with wonder and curiosity as Cain stood in front of a group of believers who followed the teachings of St. Paul and Mark. They gathered around him in a village just outside the border of what was once known as Nubia, preparing to lay siege on a small, but growing kingdom just south of where their armies camped.

"I passed through. He knew I was there and what I had come for," Cain muttered, meeting the young man's stare.

"Why were you there?" the young man pressed. "Forgive me. I do not mean to pry, it's just that…"

"For a man who knows the darkness that walks the earth, do not fear the being that has been around since the beginning. This is your chance to find the answers that you seek," Cain said, offering a smile. "Ask me."

"Coming face to face with the Son would have meant your immediate extinction," the priest stammered. "He is the Ultimate Being of Light. And you are the Ultimate Darkness."

"I am the *son* of the Ultimate Darkness," Cain corrected. "And I know. It was a risk I wanted to take. When one has existed for as long as I have, experienced the things that I have, and bore the curse for as long as I have, I wanted the one thing that humans have at their choosing."

"Which would be what?"

"Peace."

[181]

The young priest blinked several times before speaking. "And exactly how did you expect to receive that? Through death? Did you believe he would remove the curse?"

This time it was Cain's turn to pause. "He had healed so many of the diseased. He had raised the dead even, given them second chances at life without sacrifice, without pain."

"So you sought Him out?"

"Yes. I had nothing left."

"And what stopped you?"

"Apparently, I have a debt to my father." Cain seethed. "Or more like a debt to his plan. And he played a huge role in testing the legitimacy of this entity, this God in human flesh, in proving that no one can beat death except through me."

The sharp end of a silver laced sword hovered just inches from his back. Cain calmly sucked in a deep breath, unaffected by the terror-stricken expression of his current companion.

"I am going to assume that you know who I am," Cain murmured, his body as still as stone.

"We know exactly who you are, demon!" the deep voice growled behind him.

"And yet, if you truly knew who I am," Cain said slowly. "Then you would know the danger you and your men are in, even with your silver. Even with your talents."

"Wait!" screamed the priest. "You don't have to do this!"

In a move too quick for human eyes, Cain whirled around and snatched the sword from the man's grip. However, the man was prepared, and double backed before striking Cain with a psychic wave that sent him flying over the open fire pit and slamming into a nearby tree. Several quick footed men covered in dark robes emerged from the shadows after him.

"No! Don't!" the priest cried out. "Stop it! This isn't what God would want!"

"You claim to be of faith but have no clue of what God wants!" one of the warrior's spat.

"You mustn't!" the priest continues to scream as he rushed forward.

"Don't worry, my friend," Cain grumbled. "I can take care of myself." Cain's heavy palm landed a hard punch on one of the attackers, stopping him dead in his tracks. Cain laughed. "You people call yourselves the true descendants of Seth and Aklia?" Cain bellowed. "You can barely stand against me."

"We have been hunting the demons you leave behind!" roared the leader who stunned Cain with another shock wave. The leader's second in command hit the ground with his fist, causing the earth to rumble and shake. A crater opened up around Cain, causing him to lose his footing. Who were these people, he asked himself moments before he witnessed a ball of fire the size of a bull hurled in his direction. It happened too quickly for him to dematerialize to safety, and the next thing he knew, he was spiraling into a deep cavern, his body consumed with fire until he slammed onto the hard surface of the earth.

The only thing he could remember after that was darkness.

***

"We should kill him and be done with it," a voice said into Cain's subconsciousness.

"No, but the prophecy," the priest said in a hushed voice. "If you do anything to thwart what was supposed to unfold, there could be dire consequences. The Huntress might not ever be born"

That got his attention. As he awakened, he realized that they had thrown him into an iron cell. The earth beneath him singed with its blessed energies and the bars that prevented his escape had also been washed down with blessed water. None of it was strong enough to completely kill him, but he was made to be uncomfortable.

"She will be born either way," the man huffed. "This beast is not the greatest danger she is destined to face and with him gone, one less problem."

"Aklia's sword pierced his heart, and yet he lives," the priest argued.

"Good. That means it will be fun figuring out exactly what needs to be done to kill him."

Cain's growl interrupted the two, reverberating throughout the chambers. He could tell they held him beneath some sort of temple that was still under construction. "Don't you think that I should have some say in what happens to me?"

"To hell with you, demon," the leader spat, approaching Cain's cell.

"The only reason why you still stand human," Cain hissed. "Is because I will it."

"And the only reason why your head is still on your shoulders, is because I will it," the leader challenged, meeting Cain's hard stare.

"Please!" said the priest as pushed himself between Cain and the disgruntled leader. "We can work together. We know not when this Huntress might be born as we have yet to sense her presence. It has been centuries since we felt the vibration of her blade rattle the earth. But humans with gifts have been rising to meet the darkness. We are called Guardians, keepers of Light and even Sacred text."

Cain narrowed his gaze at the priest, realizing that the square little man, with the nervous gaze and sweaty palms, had been a pawn in a game the entire time.

"You sought the help of the Son, which tells me that you want redemption," the priest continued. "You want a second chance to be understood after a millennia of enduring a title that you never asked for."

"I am aware of the prophecy that both of you were murmuring about during my state of unconsciousness. You expect me to help in some way with protecting that Huntress, ensuring her survival, while at the same time condemning my own. I don't see how there is anything to be gained from this."

"A prophecy is not always set in stone," the priest stated. "Prophecies are centered around the decisions and actions of parties involved. She will hunt you if you choose to move forward with your own agenda as you have always done. But, if you choose differently, if you choose to be the opposite of what she expects you to be and aid her in the final battle that is to come, perhaps you will be rewarded with the heavenly pardon you seek. Just as we humans have a choice, so do you. You have always had a choice."

Memories that he had been long buried found their way to the surface of his mind. Memories of his brother, Abel and that single horrendous moment that reshaped his destiny forever. Had he just left, had he just walked away, things would have been different. He would have remained human and died a human man, free from the burdens that came with his curse.

"So, tell me good priest," Cain began. "What choice do I have?"

"The choice to have a new beginning," the priest offered. "The road that lies ahead makes me grateful for my limited human experience. I do not envy your immortality, for this reason nor do I envy the burden that this huntress will carry…"

"We are well aware of The Seven," the leader interrupted. "And we received word from the Archangels themselves that should you corrupt another Huntress, death would be the only thing you imagine."

"That was a mistake I will admit," Cain said tightly.

"See? He demonstrates regret!" the priest added excitedly. "This will work."

"What will work?" Cain demanded.

"Now that the God in the Flesh has paid the ultimate sacrifice, what has been hidden has been revealed. Not only are we building a temple for those who worship The Most

[186]

Holy, but also a refuge, safe haven, for those who possess gifts or talents that could best be used to serve. I'm sure you are aware that it is because of you that this world is overrun with blood drinkers and other forms of abominations. Talented people need a place to convene and to train."

As the leader whose head Cain envisioned removing from his body spoke, he had a thought. Creating a haven for the Sons and Daughters of Aklia and Seth would be the perfect trap to set for each and every one of his sibling's descendants. Here he would always know where to find them. Here, he would learn their methods and their ways, which would bring him ten steps ahead of them. And most importantly…

"And this would be the refuge for every Huntress born for not only us to protect, but for you to protect as well."

"There is a prophecy that speaks of her hunting me and bringing me to my end. You have no idea what you are asking."

"There are quite a few prophecies," the leader continued. "Most of them speak of your end. But unfortunately, there is something worse than you spoken of to be born during the end times. Unfortunately, there is no word on the outcome of this battle and this Huntress."

"And you need me to ensure her survival," Cain said dryly.

"Yes. Unless, you would rather remain at the mercy of your father, whom I am sure you are aware has moved on to a much more challenging agenda."

"Yes. His influence grows daily among the individual empires, and he has even created his own empire. He is recruiting my progeny as we speak."

"And there is also the issue of Selene," the leader added.

"What do you know of my daughter?" Cain demanded, exposing his dagger like fangs. The priest backed away, while the Guardian remain unfazed.

"She has gained power with the Romans," the head Guardian said. "She must be doing well."

Cain mulled over his current set of options: he could kill both of them and go on about his way. In time, he was certain that he would find the huntress on his own and Fate would step in from there. But then again, if he could somehow rewrite the prophecy to his benefit, he pictured a new Genesis of vampire that possessed not only the skills and strengths that defined him, but all of the skills and strengths of the huntress. And these members of his royal family would be linked by blood through birth, and not bite.

"You do know that if you kill us it, will not change the scope of the prophecy. You will seal it with our blood," the head Guardian continued.

Cain glared at the head Guardian, irritated by the male's presence. "I will offer my assistance in the construction of the safe haven. My progeny have grown rampant and uncontrollable and balance must be restored to the earth before there is another cleansing. I will even offer teachings to those who will be joining the ranks of your fighters because there will be blood drinkers who may not know who their true father is, but are nearly as old, and they will come. When the shadowy empires of the world learn of this haven's existence, they will come. But you must do something for me."

The priest looked nervously at the head Guardian, whose expression remained unreadable, his gaze moving between Cain and the Guardian, until the Guardian finally spoke.

"What?"

Cain smiled. "Find me a witch who has powerful spell work. I need not my father tracking me throughout the centuries as he has his own dubious agenda, and before you tune your lips to denying such an abominable request, do keep in mind that even in the holiest of holy temples is a congregation filled with saints and sinners."

"I am sure we can find one," the priest said quickly.

"Good. And one more thing."

"Yes?" the priest asked.

"Remove my name from the archives. Tell no one that I was here." Cain closed his eyes and became mist, riding the airwaves to freedom. He smiled to himself at the bargain he just made with a Son of Aklia, knowing full well that there would be nothing she could do to stop this brilliant plan.

Whenever this prophesied Huntress appeared, whether it be a year from now, or one million years from now, his legacy as his father had promised many centuries ago, would still stand. He allowed the wind to carry him a great distance before he returned to his physical form, just beyond the borders of Rome. There was a great deal of cleanup he needed to do on behalf of his ruthlessly savage daughter. He could smell the blood all the way from here. Guardians were more than likely tracking her or planning to stage an attack, and as much as his wayward daughter brought him much pain, she was the last source of his joy. She would bring him ruin before anything else, that he knew, but the last traces of Luluwa remained in her blood, and as long as she lived, so did Luluwa.

"Dear child," he whispered into the night. "What have you done?"

***

"We hide nothing," the Head Guardian declared through clenched teeth. "He will not be able to find his name in the archives, but every Guardian will know. We will create a separate text and only the select few will know the truth. But until then, let's go find this witch. We have much work to do."

Chapter Thirty- Four

Cain stood at the top of Mount Sinai admiring the far
reaching the rays of the sun as it extended as it retreated
beneath the horizon. Moments like this reminded him of his
gratitude for not being banished from the sun. His children
born of blood had been afforded the luxuries of both
worlds, but those born of bite suffered greatly.

Sunlight incinerated them, human food could not sustain
them, and they were driven to madness by their thirst for
human blood, and yes immortality was a gift to them as
they were frozen in time in their bodies. At whatever age
the victim sustained the bite, would be the age the victim
would exist in forever. He contemplated some of the
reckless behaviors of his cursed sons and daughters
throughout the ages: a five year old given the kiss of death;
an old crone rising from the dirt with a pair of fangs that
were the only set of teeth that sprung out from her gums,
and those weren't even the worst case scenarios. He put the
child down himself and even hunted the culprit responsible.
It stung to have to eliminate one of his own by his hand, but
certain atrocities would have almost certainly guaranteed
more angelic intervention. New entities were bred and
created throughout the course of human history and in turn,
he would learn that his kind were not the only apex
predators that hunted from the shadows, or even that
blended into the fabric of humanity.

There was a time or two of when what he thought was just
a mad wolf, but in time he learned that the painful cries
came from something other than just the lonely howl at the
moon. Other immortals existed, some dangerous, preying
on the weak and the vulnerable, while others opted to only
enjoy the pleasures that humanity had to offer. A war was

[191]

coming. What he experienced during his seemingly endless existence had been mere battles in preparation for what was to come. Soon, sides would have to be chosen and weapons drawn as heaven and earth collided in a war that had been long promised after a millennium of standoff.

"Makes you wonder if all of this was worth it in the end, doesn't it?" came the melodious voice that was a key figure in all of the madness. The entity appeared in human form this time, taking on the appearance of a middle-aged field worker, his skin dark like a toasted walnut from the sun. His eyes were the same: colorless, but with an endless darkness that he often masked with a smile.

"You always know where to find me," Cain muttered without giving him another look.

"Of course I do. You are of my blood."

Cain sighed. "What do you want?"

"That was brilliant of you to convince them trusting you to protect both the school and church... But I fear that you have divulged too many dark secrets to workers of Light."

"There has to be balance," Cain said quickly. "Have you, The Fallen Star, forgotten that? Too many blood drinkers, too many plagues against humanity, and there will be another Genesis."

"I understand balance more than you can imagine," he quipped. "I am the balance. I am the Great Test as I go 'to and fro' about the earth', but I am not here to talk about me."

"Then why are you here?" Cain asked gruffly.

"You still owe me, son," he continued. "Your stupidity and naivety cost me dearly on more than one occasion. I protected you because you lack the foresight into what is to come even a thousand years from now. "

"You need me," Cain growled, whipping his head around to face the man who regarded him with little emotion. "You need me to assist you with whatever diabolical and selfish schemes you have. Your feud is with those in the heavens. Not me."

"How can you not stand with me when your quarrel is also with those that sit on High? You were rejected since birth."

"Because of your blood."

"You soul was still allowed entry into this earth realm. You could have been a stillborn and the sin that tainted your mother would have died with you."

"What are you saying?"

"You are here because I will it so," he said calmly. "And you will remain here until I say you do not. You are free to pursue your own agenda, which ultimately is mine. Your desire to cocreate with the next Huntress, to manifest your own version of Genesis is interesting. Whatever comes of this will fit perfectly with my end game. Your progeny has nearly filled my dark realms to capacity. Souls, raw sources of life energy, and countless numbers of them have given me what I needed and now all I have to do is wait."

"For what?"

His smile widened, fueling Cain's ire. "For Fate to move its hand."

"I tire of your games," Cain hissed.

[193]

"And to think that this is only the beginning." He chuckled. "You son are my most perfect creation and from you a living plague has nearly brought humanity to its knees. My brothers have worked overtime to aid those who are still in good standing. Those innocent souls who have yet to relinquish their souls for just a shred of relief. Yet, the one thing that infuriated me when my brothers came for you is your unwillingness to stand and fight."

"Are you insane? You expect me to stand against an Archangel? And risk being smote on sight?"

"Yes, they are quite powerful but if they are as powerful as you believe them to be then why are you still standing? As a matter of fact, why is there a prophecy of a single female – the only being capable of slaying you?" He paused as his question began to sink in. "Your bite can transform humans into your likeness, the ultimate kiss of death. And in turn these same creations can do the same, replicating your likeness until the final death finds them. Imagine what it could do to a being of Light?"

"No…"

"So with all of that being said, you owe me. "

"I owe you nothing!"

"You owe me everything, including the very soul that is trapped in that cursed body of yours. For now, I will allow you time to play your games and feed your ego. But you will join me when the war comes. And whatever harem you create – everything you possess, every step you take, every vampire you make should the day you find yourself crowned as king of the heavens, all of it will be mine."

Cain opened his mouth to speak but the entity disappeared as if he never stood in front of him, sparking his rage. Cain sucked in another deep breath before releasing a roar that made the ground beneath him quake. The sun had finally retreated and the first of the evening stars made their appearance. Since his birth, he craved to belong in a world that never understood him, never considered to give him a second chance, and never saw him as anything more than a monster.

The only pair of eyes that ever wrapped him in the warmth of her love was Luluwa. Eliana had loved him as did Nunka, Tati, and Tyre. Selene, on the other hand, had grown to be too spoiled and selfish to love anyone or anything other than herself. His precious Seven, Kali and Kara, certainly still cared for him. But the love that others had for him had disappeared over time. And those who loved him were long dead or gone, and here was another moment in history where he stood to face the world alone.

He was nothing more than a tool, a weapon to use win an endless battle.

A new awareness dawned on his as a gentle breeze pushed through his locks. He learned since the beginning that timing was everything. This was how his father had existed as long as he had and why the world spun at his command. He would never again allow his fate to be determined, nor held in the hands of those deemed powerful.

His father had always said this was a game, and it was a game that he played to win. There was room for only one god in this kingdom of darkness and he would be known by only one name.

Cain.

Chapter Thirty- Five

Aklia stared out into the heavens from her post just outside the barrier, otherwise known as The Veil, and watched as an entity older than Time itself unfolded into the form of a fire bird. It all seemed to happen in slow motion as the fiery entity spread out its ever reaching wings, stretching out its monolithic form, and in a blur, a bluish white orb of energy whizzed past where she stood, and paused in front of The Phoenix. She watched as both the orb of energy and The Phoenix became one in a slow convergence of two powerful energies, until The Phoenix was completely absorbed by this unusual ball of light.

"What is happening?" she heard herself ask out loud, unsure if she should she be alarmed and notify the warrior angels, or if she should relax and allow Fate to take place. The Phoenix had existed long before the Heavens were created and she had come to know this special bird quite well. Known as the Great Protector of Time and Fate, this female energy acted as the sentinel to heaven's gates, preventing those who were considered The Fallen from returning. But now, Heaven's greatest champion was abandoning its post, and for what?

"It is time," came a soft baritone of the Archangel known as Gabriel from behind.

Aklia turned around to face the colorless stare of the winged spirit. "Time for what?" Aklia asked.

"The Prophecy." Gabriel said pointedly. "Your descendant is on her way to earth as we speak."

"Wait," Aklia said looking back at where The Phoenix once rose. "That cannot be."

"Yes. This time dear, Aklia, she will not fail."

"She mustn't go down now," Aklia protested, holding her face, and staring in the direction of the blue-red energy that headed straight for earth. "He knows too much. He has learned entirely too much. We should just wait until after the Second Coming."

"We cannot wait. And it is promised that she will succeed. Only one prophecy stands in truth."

Aklia extended her hand and almost instantly, her blade materialized. "We need to go down and protect her. If he finds her."

"He won't. He knows that the time is close to her birth, but he will not find her just yet. She will grow as a regular human for most of her childhood and when it is time for the Guardians to find her, she will without a doubt send out an energy signature that her assigned Guardian will recognize. She will be hidden in plain sight. He will hunt her, yes. But rest assured he won't find her as quickly as he would like to. He will hunt down whatever human appears special while our huntress grows in peace, learning the world around her as any human would. This is the plan."

"But she will need to be trained as soon as possible!" Aklia protested. "My daughters held their first weapons as soon as they could walk. There is so much training she will have to undergo to prepare for the dark road she must travel."

"All will be well, Aklia," Gabriel promised.

"I must follow the soul."

[197]

"No. You will stay here until it is time. Her spirit guides are tracking her soul and will follow her for the entirety of her life. They will lead her Primary Guardian to her."

"But I—"

"No. You have been ordered by The Most High to stay put. She is different and is nothing like the Huntresses that came before her, including you. Have faith."

Gabriel disappeared, leaving Aklia alone to watch the orb until it vanished in the earth realm, So this was the plan from the Most High, she thought to herself with disbelief. To leave perhaps the most powerful huntress ever born to Fate. To delay her powers to protect her identity? What about her family? How would they protect her? What if Fate took a cruel turn and her mother, father, and whatever siblings she might have, fell victims to Darkness? To not know the female's identity at least, disturbed her to no end.

As long as Cain still lived, Aklia vowed to do everything in her power to protect this new Huntress. She had failed too many of them over the centuries, and this time was promised to be the final birth of the Huntress line. The line, the legacy, all of it, would end with her.

"Please God, let her survive, " Aklia whispered, still clutching her blade. "Let no harm befall her. Don't let us lose another one, please."

***

Chapter Thirty-Six

Vatican City, Rome 2016

She is here, Cain thought to himself as he circled the perimeter of the campus, unbeknownst to the Guardians who manned the towers and walked amongst the students and staff that flooded the concrete. *After many centuries of searching, of waiting, she is finally here.* Her energy signature had increased in strength since her arrival at the school. Her powers were finally blossoming and her scent... she smelled like sweet honey and milk, a divine combination. At first, he only received impressions of her, nothing but dark silhouettes of her image. He spent many a night fantasizing about her, imagining what her will would be like. Would she break as easily as the others who had come before her? Would she be strong enough to refuse him? What weaknesses did she possess that he could exploit?

And which individual here at the Academy had been chosen to be her Primary Guardian?

He gathered up his molecular form and rode the airwaves back to his lair just outside the city. Soon she would grow in strength and skill, and it would be then that he would introduce himself to her world, but not as an enemy. As a friend. He learned many times over what the essential core of a Huntress was composed of, but if given the wrong set of circumstances, if he could separate her mind from her emotions, he could then gain access to the more important thing, her soul.

This Huntress in particular did not have an easy childhood filled with love and support. She wasn't even raised to know what she was, which was an interesting play on the part of the Light, yet her energy grew stronger each day. And there was something else about her that he could not quite put his finger on, but he knew he would soon figure it out. He could hear her now in his mind, training to yield a sword – Aklia's sword.

"Rider!" he heard her call out.

Wood met wood and he cringed when he sensed her opponent gain the upper hand and knock her off her feet.

My beautiful, Huntress, he thought to himself. *You still have so much to learn. And soon I will be the one to teach you.*

Without so much as another thought, he continued to propel himself forward, riding high above the city, enjoying the clear blue sky, the crisp breeze, and the magnificent view of the skyline. He looked down to see droves of humans, moving about in their day to day lives, most of them unaware of the fact that monsters, the very creatures that they fictionalized to the backdrops of their nightmares, actually did exist. And the humans that did learn of the truth of the existence of monsters, did so by unfortunate circumstances.

How many lives had he been responsible for the ending since the inception of his curse? Hundreds of thousands? Millions? The cosmic debt that he owed the Universe was far too great for him to count. But even in the end, he figured he would still stand. He held many bounties on his head, most of them from his father. At some point, the day would come when he would have to stand against the very entity that started this entire line of tragedy, not for righteous purposes, but for his own freedom.

Free us, came the whispers in his mind. *Free us, Son of the Fallen Star. Free us, and we will serve you.*

In due time, he mentally shot back to the trapped entities. His father thought he had everyone, and everything wrapped around his wicked finger. Cain chuckled at the thought. If only The Beast knew.

He materialized in full form onto his balcony, his thoughts drifting towards the memories of his earlier days with his beloved wife Luluwa. Images of her beautiful, round face, once filled with life and hope for the future with him and only him, nearly brought tears to his eyes. Life had been cruel to him since birth, and even crueler with Time. Could it be that Time was his true enemy? That Aklia and her descendants and all of the brave humans that dared to stand against him were really just pawns set up to stand against him? And for the billionth time, he had to ask himself, why him? Why was his soul chosen to walk this path of darkness, only to be punished for the decisions made for survival?

"Oh, Luluwa," he moaned, covering his face with his hands. "My beautiful, sweet Luluwa. I wish you were here with me."

As per usual, his cries fell on deaf ears. He plopped down on his black leather sectional. An icy chill filled his spirit, followed an image of a distant progeny being dusted by a Guardian.

"Fucking roaches," he muttered as the chill began to fade. The image of the dark- haired Guardian disappeared just as quickly as it appeared. Soon, he promised himself, he would return to the world's forefront, as he had centuries ago. It took many battles, defeats, and losses to learn the importance of patience. One step made prematurely could ruin everything and tip the scales of balance in the favor of his father, or worse, the Light, where his sister resided.

This new Huntress would either be the key to his undoing, or his beginning.

"Let the games begin," he said out loud.

Keep reading for a sneak peek into book 5 of *The Vampire Hunters Academy, The Forsaken.*

The Forsaken – Sneak Peak

The hot humid terrain of what was once known as the Fertile Crescent no longer possessed the rich, vibrant beauty that Cain remembered from back in the days of Eden. Desecrated. Babylon had been desecrated, century after century. The Hanging Gardens that once graced the temples of King Solomon had been a sight. Kings and Queens of renown once flocked to Babylon to partake of the glory that was once the epicenter of mankind. The fertile banks of the Euphrates and the Tigris had irrigated the crops, keeping the citizens within the gates well fed and the marketplace flourishing. He recalled traipsing through there a time or two, even gaining the favor of King Solomon himself. He could have easily taken the city from the wise king's grasp, but he was still being hunted by the archangels, and doing so would have guaranteed his demise.

Now as he stared at what was left of the ruins, Cain shook his head, fighting back the painful memories that he preferred to keep locked away in a black box tucked deep in the caverns of his mind. But it would be here where it began that it would soon end. He heard them loud and clear. Their mournful cries. Their pleas for redemption. Their pain. And soon he would be their savior.

But just how did Daemon know exactly where to find them? How would an ordinary vampire, born of bite and not blood figure out the location of The Fallen? This was information designed only for those of angelic bloodline or had been blessed with the knowledge. He would soon find out. Cain walked casually, making note of the few scattered humans that had been displaced due to the bombing. Their tattered clothing, battered faces and hopeless expressions made him smile. When all was done, humanity would bow before him. This world would be his alone and the angels in heaven would abandon it, leaving humans to his mercy.

And with the help of The Fallen, he would entomb The Beast in the very place his brethren had suffered for well over a millennia.

"Help us..." came the pained raspy whisper in the wind.

"Set us free..." came another mournful wail.

He smiled as he approached the site that contained entities as ancient as time itself. The invisible barrier that blanketed the perimeter felt like a laser hot knife slicing through his skin. This was definitely it. Humans instinctively avoided the area, most of them repulsed by the dreadful feeling or those with wickedness in their souls became ten times more twisted than before. Here lied the presence of pure evil. They'd fallen from the grace and mercy of above, completely and forever separated from the Creator and no place to call home.

If The Beast only knew...

Cain fought through the pain of crossing the barrier, and once inside he surveyed the barren field that surrounded him. What was left of the great city of Babylon stood no more, but perhaps with their help he could rebuild it. Slowly he uncurled his fist and using his index finger he willed his nail to grow into a sharp talon. Without a second thought he sliced through his palm and watched with indifference as the blood pooled and then dripped onto the scorching hot ground. He waited to see what would come of it, studying his blood as it seeped into the dry surface. But soon, the earth began to tremble, splintering in half, forcing Cain to jump back several feet, thrusting him into the invisible barrier. For miles it seemed, the earth cracked and split, separating itself until a wide crater formed, swallowing what was left of the ruins. The wails and the moaning stopped, and Cain found himself standing, overlooking the edge of a trench that stretched deep into the underground.

He listened for signs of movement, debating if he should take the plummet to the bottom until suddenly four pairs of massive black wings shot out of the cavern, knocking Cain flat on his back. A dark shadow temporarily eclipsed the sun as the figures took flight into the air, and for a moment, regret claimed him. He watched in a daze as the entities landed in front of him. Each stood over six feet with hard colorless eyes staring directly at him. Their expressions, unreadable as he quickly jumped to his feet.

"Vampire," said the largest of The Fallen. His eyes narrowed as he took in the image of Cain standing before him. "Cursed. You dare set us free? Angels? Beings higher than yourself, entities of realms you could only imagine?"

"Mayhap he wishes for extermination," said the other that donned a snow white mohawk.

"From where I stand," Cain growled. "All of you are just as damned as I- perhaps far worse actually. The murder of my own blood condemned me to my fate. But you violated the highest of orders, which led to your unfortunate incarceration."

"We should kill you where you stand," the larger Fallen threatened.

"And then what?" Cain challenged. "This world is foreign to you. New technology that supersedes that of what you built eons ago, including weapons. Humans are no longer spiritual creatures that bend to the concept of worship. They worship themselves, following the very path that The Beast had paved at humanity's birth. Their souls are just about primed and ready for The Beast's plans as

[205]

prophesized. All of this transpired while you all remained trapped beneath the surface of the earth. Blind to sensation but craving it. Thirsty but unable to drink. Starving but unable to feed. And here I stand, a vampire, able to move as I choose…and here I am the very thing that you hate, but the same thing that gave you freedom."

The four entities glared back at Cain; their eyes filled with raw hatred. Cain waited, anticipating an immediate violent response from the larger of the group that would surely be his end. But seconds ticked by, and the entity remained as stoic as a statue.

"What do you want?" The larger of the fallen began. "It is apparent that we are in your debt. Name your price vampire."

Cain smiled, exposing his massive fangs with pride. "Pledge your fealty to me and the world is yours for the taking."

Four pairs of colorless eyes blackened instantly. The temperature surrounding them dropped from scorching heat levels to an icy chill.

"We will do no such thing!" Said the one with the mohawk. "We will raze the planet ourselves, with no help from you-"

"If that is what you wish," Cain continued calmly. "But duly note that I am quite certain that the warrior angels are preparing for an attack as we speak. I did however break the Veil."

When The Fallen fell silent, Cain knew he had won. It was just a matter of time before they agreed to submit to his leadership, and then it would be The Beast himself who would be on the run.

[206]

"If we pledge our allegiance to you, what will that grant us?" The Fallen with the most beautifully exquisite face Cain had ever seen on a male. Smooth rich skin, sensual lips and a perfect nose on a handsomely chiseled face nearly masked by a head full of rich blonde hair that fell well beyond his shirtless back.

"You are free to move about as you please. But for now, all that I ask of you is to lay low for a while. Blend in with the humans-I can teach you how to do that. But what I need you for is to help me incarcerate The Beast," Cain admitted.

"You dare us to challenge one of our own?" The larger Fallen gasped.

"Do not pretend to have a code of ethics given where I just freed you," Cain snapped. "Stand with me or stand the chance of Michael leading his squadron to finish off what they started a millennia ago."

"Fine," said Mohawk. "But on one condition."

"And what is that?" Cain asked.

"You are to free the others," Mohawk continued. "There are hundreds of us locked away at various locations around the globe."

Cain considered the request. More Fallen meant a larger army to accomplish his goals. There was nothing more to consider. He was done hiding and with his new army, he would soon acquire the one thing that would make his millennia long life worth living again: Sanaya.

"Done."

The Fallen Angels that surrounded him dropped to a knee and kneeled before Cain, acknowledging him as their leader. A new era in leadership had just begun. The

[207]

Darkness would soon be led by Cain and his Fallen troops, and Babylon would be rebuilt to its former glory.

And he would call his army: The Forsaken.

Check out the entire series of The Vampire Hunters Academy!

The Darkness

The Shadows

The Reckoning

The Cursed

The Forsaken

Cain

Coming Soon...

The Book of Maya

About the Author:

Delizhia Jenkins is an Urban Fantasy and Paranormal Romance author who currently resides in Inglewood, CA. The love for writing began in elementary school when the passion for storytelling developed into a journey of writing. Over the years, she honed her craft for storytelling and the written word by excelling in subjects such English and English Literature; and by indulging in her favorite past time which involved reading the works of Anne Rice, K'Wan, Christopher Pike, Carl Weber, Omar Tyree and finally the late L.A. Banks. J.R. Ward's *Black Dagger Brotherhood* also claimed her heart and author Karen Marie Moning joined the ranks of Miss Jenkins' all-time favorite authors.

Miss Jenkins began publishing in 2013 with her first African American romance novel, *Love at Last.* After that, it was realized that her true magic rested in her writing about the ancient, the esoteric, and the supernatural. Moreover, since 2014, after her release of Nubia Rising: The Awakening, Miss Jenkins remained true to herself and her calling. And of course, being a true romantic at heart, it was important for her to fuse romance with the paranormal with a dash of "color." Miss Jenkins prides herself on writing for "the woman without the fairytale" and of course bringing magic and melanin to each book she writes.

Follow Miss Jenkins on the following platforms:

Instagram: @miss_jenkins_books

Twitter: @septembershope or hunters_vampire

Website: missjenkinsbooks.com

Manufactured by Amazon.ca
Bolton, ON